ENEMY ON HER HOSPITAL WARD

SUE MACKAY

MEDICAL ROMANCE

Recycling programs for this product may not exist in your area

ISBN-13: 978-1-335-99370-0

Enemy on Her Hospital Ward

For questions and comments about the quality of this book, please contact us at CustomerService@Harlequin.com.

Harlequin Enterprises ULC
22 Adelaide St. West, 41st Floor
Toronto, Ontario M5H 4E3, Canada
www.Harlequin.com

HarperCollins Publishers
Macken House, 39/40 Mayor Street Uppe
Dublin 1, D01 C9W8, Ireland
www.HarperCollins.com

Printed in U.S.A.

1 2 3 4 5 6 7 8 9 10 HDC 28 27 26 25

Glancing at Tamara, he saw a flicker of surprise cross her face.

So she still thought he was that arrogant guy she'd known before. *Thanks a lot, Tamara. You sure know how to rub in the past.* He probably deserved it, but still. "It's the right thing to do for both Joena and her patient," he snapped.

Tamara locked her eyes on him. "It is. I like that you understand. Not all doctors do."

At least she hadn't denied what she'd been thinking. His tension backed off. "Seems I'm not beyond surprising you." There might be more surprises to come, hopefully good ones.

Her eyes widened, then she smiled. A genuine smile aimed totally at him. "Seems you could be right."

He'd take those smiles anytime. They lightened his heart and made him feel good about everything. "Right, let's get on with delivering a baby. What a way to start our time here."

"The best, I reckon."

As long as nothing went wrong, he would agree with Tamara on that.

Dear Reader,

When Tamara and Fergus find out they're working together as volunteers at Vanuatu Hospital, the last thing either expect is for their attraction to each other from college to flare up even hotter than before. Back then, they'd had some serious disagreements that kept them from indulging in each other.

Now they find there's so much more to like about one another than purely physical. But Tamara can't trust Fergus not to trash her as he once did. After facing a huge crisis during his last year at college that Tamara is aware of, he's not sure he can risk getting close and letting her in. She knows too much about him, and it's not all good.

But there's no denying the sparks are flying between them, and when Vanuatu is decimated by an earthquake, nothing can stop them from getting together physically, which helps all their hangups fall away. Until it's time to return home and then reality sets in. Can theses two find their HEA? Or will they return to the lonely lives they'd both had before this adventure?

I hope you enjoy finding out.

All the best,

Sue MacKay

Sue MacKay lives with her husband in New Zealand's beautiful Marlborough Sounds, with the water on her doorstep and the birds and the trees at her back door. It is the perfect setting to indulge her passions of entertaining friends by cooking them sumptuous meals, drinking fabulous wine, going for hill walks or kayaking around the bay—and, of course, writing stories.

Books by Sue MacKay

Harlequin Medical Romance

Stranded with the Paramedic
Single Mom's New Year Wish
Brought Together by a Pup
Fake Fiancée to Forever?
Resisting the Pregnant Pediatrician
Marriage Reunion with the Island Doc
Paramedic's Fling to Forever
Healing the Single Dad Surgeon
Brooding Vet for the Wallflower
Wedding Date with the ER Doctor
Parisian Surgeon's Secret Child
A Fling with the ER Doc

Visit the Author Profile page
at Harlequin.com for more titles.

To all the medical staff and volunteers driving vans
and providing other necessities, a huge thank you
for being there for my husband. You all rock.
—Sue MacKay

CHAPTER ONE

TAMARA FROST SCANNED the people waiting to board the flight to Vanuatu. There he was, standing talking to a couple in casual summer-weight clothes, looking as striking as ever. More so if she was seeing clearly. The other two people were likely who she'd also be working alongside. As for Mr Full of Himself, her mouth tightened around her old name for him. She would not let Fergus Collier get to her with his arrogant attitude. It might've been many years since their college ball when his friends had found them kissing and been derogatory about her wearing a thrift shop dress, but she hadn't forgotten. Fergus hadn't joined in with their mockery, but nor had he stepped up for her despite the sparks firing between them after a mind-blowing kiss.

He'd always been able to wind her up in a blaze of heat with his steady, grey-eyed gaze whenever she saw him. When he'd asked her to go to the ball with him, she'd turned him down flat, despite fancying him like crazy. He ran with the wealthy, privileged crowd who only dated the beautiful, popular girls, one after another, whereas she and her friends were the quiet, study-hard group. Turning him down had taken all her willpower, but she'd refused to become just another of Fergus's dating statistics.

On the night of the ball, she'd stepped outside to take a breath of air and get away from seeing Fergus dancing with every pretty girl available while deliberately ignoring her. He'd rattled her more than ever that night, and when he'd followed her outside, taking her hands and locking his intense gaze on her, sparks had ignited. And when he'd leaned down to kiss her, all resistance had flown out of her head. Pressing into him as his mouth took hers, not in a demanding, see-what-you've-been-missing way, but in a gentle, giving, almost careful way. Her first proper kiss. One she still remembered to this day—along with the humiliation that had followed. 'Want to dance with me out here, instead?' he'd whispered. 'Please,' she'd groaned in reply. Then his mates had bowled out through the door, laughing and joking, and surrounded them, teasing Fergus, taunting her about her cheap dress. And he'd hesitated, then stepped away from her.

It had taken a couple of attempts to lift her shoulders as though she didn't care, and tell Fergus he was an arrogant arse who didn't deserve her, before turning and heading inside to join her true friends. But she had done it—stood up to him in front of his disgusting mates. That was what mattered. Not the pain and mortification of being ignored, the embarrassment over her cheap dress and how worthless she'd been made to feel.

She was still staring at Fergus now, almost wishing she hadn't come.

Right then he glanced around and instantly spotted her. His face gave nothing away, as though he'd been on the lookout for her and was prepared for anything she might say. Surprise, Fergus. She wasn't here to talk about him to him, or to anyone else. What had happened between them in the past was well and truly behind her, she decided, though she couldn't help feeling a little cautious since she didn't know him anymore and would be working alongside him during the coming weeks. Who knew what was going on behind that same decimating gaze? If only she wasn't so aware of him!

When she'd seen his name on the list of medical people heading to Port Vila to help the island locals for a month, she'd briefly considered pulling out of the volunteer programme, but more than anything she wanted to help the people there. Besides, Fergus was in her past. He hadn't ruined her life by not supporting her when his mates had jeered that they reckoned her op-shop dress was deliberately two sizes too small just so she could flaunt her pathetic figure. One of her friends—no longer a friend—had even joined in the teasing, just because she'd been jealous Fergus had asked Tamara to the ball. Tamara knew if anything good had come from that night, it was that she'd learned never to let anyone treat her like mud on their shoes ever again.

Dodging around people and carry-on bags, she headed over to the small group. 'Hello, Fergus.' She held out her hand to shake his. 'Seems it's a small world as far as you and I are concerned.'

His head jerked back a fraction as though she'd surprised him.

Good.

Get over yourself, Tamara. You're tough. He can't hurt you anymore. Then why was she feeling so uncomfortable? She couldn't still fancy him after all this time. That'd be plain weird. It had been a lusty teen crush, that's all, not something that had stuck with her in the intervening years.

Fergus reached to shake her hand with a cool, firm grip. 'Hello, Tamara. It was a surprise to see your name on the list for this trip. I didn't know you'd become a nurse.' He looked genuinely impressed.

She blinked. Where was the arrogance? The hubris? He was a doctor, after all, and the Fergus she'd known would've rubbed her face in that fact. 'I hadn't expected to see yours either.' Helping people in a small country with few medical resources didn't match the guy she'd once known, but she knew life had thrown a huge curve ball his way during his final few weeks at college. His father had been arrested and then imprisoned for scamming millions of dollars from people under the guise of an investment company he'd set up. When the wealthy lifestyle he'd been living had disappeared overnight, Fergus's outlook on life must've taken a huge knock. Maybe he'd gained some understanding of those less fortunate than he'd once been. She shrugged. Time would tell. 'Nursing was always my dream, right from the time I understood I'd have to get a job when I grew up.'

'I didn't know that.' He stopped, suddenly looking off balance. So unlike him!

'I don't suppose you did.' Why would he? They hadn't sat around talking and getting to know each other, merely ogled one another whenever they were in the same space, getting hot and confused. Well, she had, anyway. He'd been used to girls drooling over him. Especially at rugby games where he was captain of the college First Fifteen and played as a forward, with his rugby shorts emphasising a very sexy backside and muscular thighs.

'Tamara, I'm sorry, I'm being rude. I don't believe you've met Tim and Sarah McPherson. They're the other half of the team.' He smiled at the couple getting to their feet.

Turning to them, she smiled easily. 'It's nice to meet you both. You're from Hamilton?' So the notes said, but it didn't hurt to check.

'We are.' Sarah returned her smile. 'We've got a surgical practice there. Like you, I'm a nurse while Tim does the easy work.'

Tim grinned. 'You said it, babe.'

Sarah asked Tamara, 'Have you done this sort of work before?'

'Volunteering in offshore communities? No, this is a first for me and I'm really looking forward to it. You and Tim?'

'It's our second time. Unlike Fergus here. He's been to a fair few countries on the volunteer's scheme. Haven't you, Fergus?'

He was turning out to be nothing like she'd expected. If only he didn't still ramp up the heat when he looked at her. 'Have you been to Vanuatu before?' she asked him to distract herself from that rather disturbing thought.

'No, this is my first time. I've heard the locals are wonderful to get along with.' No smile for her.

Did she still annoy him? Strange how she hoped not. She shouldn't care. But then again, she wanted this to be a great trip with no complications. Getting along with Fergus would help with that. 'Sounds great.'

The speakers crackled to life. 'Ladies and gentlemen, we're about to begin boarding flight five oh one to Port Vila, starting with business class and families with small children.'

Here we go. A fizz of excitement tickled Tamara. She was starting an adventure unlike anything she'd done before. The time had come to get out there and do something completely different in a place where she'd normally have gone to the resorts. Not because she was a snob, but when she took leave from work, all she usually wanted to do was unwind and relax. Not once had she known this sense of excitement filling her, though. Excitement that had nothing to do with Fergus. What could be better than a working holiday looking after people in need of medical attention? Nursing was in her blood, her way of looking out for others without getting too involved in their lives.

Except over the previous few months, when she'd been nursing her father as he battled with stage four bowel cancer. A battle he'd lost. It had been a very close and personal time, which had taken a lot out of her. But not for a moment did she regret taking an extended leave of absence from work and being there for her dad. Looking after the man who'd been there for her and her sister, Sashi, all their lives, especially after their mother died when a van had crossed the road in front of the long-haul truck she'd been driving. In an attempt to avoid the van, her mother had swerved to the roadside, which gave way, causing the truck to roll down the bank. Her mother had been crushed in the cab by the container on the back.

'Coming?' Fergus asked with a hint of amusement.

'What?'

'They've called our rows to board.'

He knew her seat number? 'Sorry, I was miles away.'

'Obviously.' A genuine smile came her way, not as relaxed and friendly as what he'd given the other two, but she'd accept it.

You haven't been very forthcoming, either. True. Working with Fergus would be awkward if she didn't do everything possible to turn things around enough to get along with him without complications. He appeared to have changed somewhat since they'd left college. It must've been incredibly hard to face everyone after what his father had done. The story had been headline news across New Zealand for weeks. Just about everyone in Nelson had something to say on the subject, true or not. Her stomach knotted for Fergus. How had he come through that while still managing to look sane and sensible? It wouldn't have been easy by any stretch, when he'd never held back about his wonderful lifestyle. Had he truly changed or just become better at hiding his arrogant nature? Until she knew for certain, she'd cut him some slack.

'Let's do this.' She joined the queue of people getting their boarding passes scanned and waited her turn. She'd been overreacting to the heat he caused to roll through her, letting old memories from long ago get in the way of sanity. A waste of time and energy. They might become friends, but that was as far as it'd go. She didn't trust men anymore—for very good reasons, she reminded herself.

She turned to look at Fergus standing behind her. He hadn't boarded with the business-class passengers, which once would've been a given. Now that he'd matured into a man, he was better looking than ever. There was a new quietness about him, along with a steadiness that suggested he'd settled into a life that suited him. A life where he wasn't handed everything on a plate? A life where he didn't rub other people's noses in his wealth and privilege? Even as a doctor, he probably wasn't anywhere near as well off as he used to be. His father's money and properties had all been seized so money could be returned to those who'd believed Jim Collier would make them a big profit. No one got all their investments back, though. There'd also been rumours that Collier had hidden most of his ill-gotten gains, but that had never been proven, and then he'd died in prison some years later, after a short illness. From the odd comment she'd heard from friends, Fergus had apparently turned his back on his father and made his own way through university and medical school. If so, it said a lot about how much he'd changed—something she admired. It would've taken guts and sheer determination to get where he was today.

Fergus followed Tamara down the aisle to their seats, unable to ignore how those cream Capri pants accentuated her curvy backside. Some things hadn't changed. His mouth dried as he placed his bag in the overhead locker then reached for hers. Seemed she could still get to him, even after all this time. 'Let me do that for you.'

'I can manage.'

'I'm sure you can.' He tugged at her backpack and smiled to himself when she finally loosened her grip and got a book out of the side pocket before handing it over. 'We're in the middle seats, Tim and Sarah beside us.' For the next three hours he had to sit alongside this woman who'd intermittently messed with his mind for years whenever he thought about his past. She'd made him so damned confused at times because he didn't know how to face the mix of emotions she caused in him. Had always caused.

He'd longed to learn all there was to know about her. She'd kept the same friends throughout college, had fought for them if someone hurt them, something he hadn't done for her, hence him deserving her vitriol. He used to get a kick out of winding her up so she spat sharp words at him while her eyes gleamed bright. It was something she never seemed to do with anyone else, suggesting he got to her as much as she did him. He'd wondered from time to time what might've happened after their illicit kiss if they had danced together the night of the ball, and his friends hadn't ruined his chance of holding her in his arms for the first time.

But then a bare month later, the news about his father's scam had landed hard and heavy, and his life became unrecognisable. There'd been little room for anything but the attempt to stay upright. Thank goodness for Kelvin, because he was the only friend to stick with him throughout the horror that came after the arrest of Jim Collier.

Wealth has made you so arrogant you don't care about anything or anyone else but yourself.

Tamara's words had rattled around in his head on and off since the night he'd let his mates get away with insulting her because she couldn't afford a perfect gown for the ball. She'd come straight back at him with that, and more. She'd been hurt, then angry when he didn't stand up for her. When she'd called him arrogant, he'd shrugged and walked away. No girl had ever said that to him before. But he had started to wonder if she had a valid point. Had he become too big for his boots? Not that he'd changed how he went about getting onside with the prettiest girls so he could have fun. *That* came later, when his father was arrested for conning people out of their hard-earned money when they were looking for safe investments. Millions of dollars had disappeared somewhere offshore while *he'd* been living the life of Riley thinking nothing could touch him. Why would it have occurred to him that Jim Collier was a scammer? His father had always come across as a caring man who he'd hoped to emulate. Until he could no longer believe in that. He hadn't forgiven his father for what he'd done and never would, even though he was now dead. Hell, he still couldn't forgive himself for how readily he'd accepted what rightly wasn't his, nor his father's to give. Which was why nowadays he did whatever he could to help people in need.

Fergus sank into his seat and buckled up, his mind still on the past. The consequences of that time had been huge for everyone involved. He'd stayed in Nelson only to finish the school year, then went to Dunedin to find a job to earn enough to go to Otago University to study medicine the next year, as he'd always intended. The main difference being that before the truth came out about his father, he'd planned on going to Auckland University, a place he couldn't afford after what had happened. Not that Dunedin came cheap, but it was easier. He'd felt more comfortable there, away from the guys he knew were going to Auckland and had given him loads of grief about his father after the truth had come out. So much for trusting his so-called mates. His grandparents had supported him as much as they could throughout that time, and he'd love them forever for that. His mother left Nelson within weeks of his father's heinous crimes hitting the headlines, and had moved to Auckland, where she quickly found another rich man to live with while she waited to obtain a divorce. That was another scenario he hadn't been keen to become a part of, and when she'd offhandedly suggested he join her, he'd said no. Oh yeah, it had been an absolutely wonderful time in his life.

But he'd got through it and was proud of himself for that. Now he was heading to Vanuatu for a month to help as many as he could—along with the woman seated beside him. She obviously still had no time for him. He couldn't blame her for that, though. He'd behaved despicably towards her, and despite how long ago it had been, she had no reason to think he might've changed. The one thing he admired about Tamara was that she'd always given back as good as she'd got. So unusual. He'd never had a problem attracting female attention; girls had always flocked around him, wanting to be the one. Was that why he'd never forgotten her? Nothing to do with how she turned him on with merely a glance? Couldn't be, surely? But then he saw people differently these days to how he did back then, when he'd believed he was invincible. Now he knew only too well how untrue that was and, as Tamara had said, just how arrogant he'd been. He hated to think what he'd be like now if he hadn't been dealt such a huge lesson. It'd clearly been a necessary experience to make him turn out to be a decent guy.

Beside him Tamara opened the book she held.

He got it. Conversation was off the table. He'd have to try changing her mind about that. After all, they did have to get along well enough during the coming weeks working together. 'I see you're still living in Nelson.' The notes everyone had received about this trip included who was going, their qualifications and where they currently worked.

'I am at the moment.'

'You're a theatre nurse?'

'Currently, yes.'

'Tamara, I understand you'd rather I got off the plane and headed straight back home, but that's not going to happen.'

'I know.'

She sounded withdrawn rather than snippy, but he couldn't let it go. 'We're part of a team, one that has to at least get along.' Not necessarily totally at ease, in their case.

She sighed, closed her book and looked at him. 'You're right. I apologise for being terse. I've also spent a lot of time on surgical wards and occasionally on gynaecology.'

'All of which fits in with what we're going to be doing in Vanuatu.'

'Yes, it does. How long have you been in Auckland?'

'I moved up there after I finished training in Otago.' He and Kelvin, plus another med school friend, had decided to go into practice together once they'd qualified. They'd agreed to give Auckland a try, and it was working out well being in a large city where no one knew him or, more specifically, who his father was—unlike in Nelson, where it was impossible to be anonymous. 'I worked in various hospitals around the country while specialising. Now I live on the North Shore, where I'm a partner in an obstetrics and gynaecology practice.' The North Shore wasn't a destitute part of the city by any means, but he hadn't gone there because of the middle-class residents. There'd been a need for specialists in their field and the three of them had decided to fill the gap.

She blinked. 'Good on you.'

'Did you train in Nelson?' This was a bit like pulling teeth, but now he'd started he didn't want to stop. If they were to ever move on and maybe become friends, they had to start somewhere.

Her thick, dark blond ponytail flicked over her shoulder as she shook her head, sending his hormones into overdrive. Just like he used to react to her all those years ago. 'I got out of town and went to Wellington.'

Why had she done that? 'Needed to spread your wings?'

Was that a smile? 'Heck, yes. Most of my friends headed to university, going in all directions, and I figured that after I left school it would be the freest time of my life to do whatever and go wherever I chose.'

'Yet now you're back in Nelson.'

Her face closed down. 'Yes. It's where home is.'

Something bad had happened. It was there in the way she'd just mentally pulled back, in how her fingers tightened around her book. Not his place to ask. Anyway, he doubted she'd answer even if he did. They weren't anywhere near close enough. He'd got further than he'd expected, so it might be time to sit back and relax, make the most of whatever was on offer from Tamara. They'd both grown up in the intervening years, had long-since changed from hormonal teenagers to sensible adults. At least *he'd* become sensible. She always had been; had a part-time job at the local supermarket throughout college, and was a member of a close group of friends who'd always studied hard, so he'd bet his last month's pay she was still sensible and would take nursing very seriously. There'd always been an undercurrent of serious determination to be good at anything she did, he recalled. Even when it came to telling him where to go. A smile slid over his mouth. Intriguing, to say the least.

Pushing in an earplug, he went through the available movies. Anything to pass the hours before touchdown in Port Vila. After the plane took off, that was. The door had been closed so they couldn't be far off leaving Auckland.

'Ladies and gentlemen.' A flight attendant interrupted his thoughts.

Knowing almost word for word what she'd say, he selected a movie instead, then had to wait until she'd finished her safety spiel before he could begin watching it. While he waited his eyes drifted sideways to Tamara. She'd been a stunning girl who'd caught his attention far too often. She hadn't been one to play on her looks, though, instead coming across as wanting people to like her for who she was on the inside. Yet he doubted there'd been a guy at college who hadn't had heated thoughts about how her curvy figure filled out the clothes she wore. She was always friendly and lots of fun—except with him.

She'd become even more attractive as an adult. Not quite the same daredevil look in her eyes as there used to be, but that could be because she was currently with people she didn't know—and him. One thing he could tell her was that he was no longer arrogant. She might've been the first to say he was, but she hadn't been the last, and he'd eventually taken it on board and done something to prove everyone wrong.

After his father's transgressions came to light, his friends had been quick to tell him the same and more, when once they'd been his best buddies. It had been gut-wrenching when they'd turned their backs on him. He'd struggled getting out of bed every morning to go to college, but had forced himself to, so he could become a doctor. Other than his grandparents, that goal had kept him on track more than anything else. Grandma and Grandad had been shocked over what their son had done, and had struggled to believe he was capable of conning people out of their hard-earned savings for his own benefit. They'd had nothing more to do with him right up until his death in prison from pneumonia.

The plane began to taxi out to the runway. Fergus settled further into his seat. There was never enough room for his long legs in cattle class, but he put up with the discomfort. First class was no longer his choice. He could afford it now, but after taking it for granted when he was younger, he wasn't prepared to be seen striding down the aisle to sit in a space that back here would hold nearly two people.

So, Tamara, I have learned a few things about myself and sucked up the lemon called arrogance. But he still owed her an apology and wouldn't feel entirely at ease around her until he gave it to her. Even then he doubted he'd be comfortable around her. It wasn't possible with everything that had happened to him in the years since he first saw her playing college netball, raising his hormone levels off the chart.

'Would you like something to drink with your lunch?' the flight attendant asked Tamara as she pressed the brake on the overloaded trolley.

'A glass of bubbles, thank you.' A celebration to this new adventure despite the man sitting beside her. Who knew? They might end up getting along perfectly fine. He hadn't been unfriendly so far.

Fergus paused the movie and removed the earplug. 'Salad looks all right.'

For airline food it looked passable, but then she wasn't too picky. 'Hopefully. At least the bubbles will be enjoyable.'

'I'll have a lager, thanks,' he told the stewardess, taking the tray she passed across. 'What made you decide to come on board with the medical volunteers, Tamara?'

He was full of questions. She'd go along with it for now. Anything to make things more comfortable between them. 'I thought it might be fun to do, instead of charging off to another country to go sightseeing for days on end.'

After her father had died, she'd been lost, and

for a while had felt ambivalent about returning to her normal working life as though nothing had happened. Sashi had suggested she should get away and do something for herself. Something that meant more than having a cocktail on the beach. Something she could put her heart into.

'So I dug into information on medical volunteers, and here I am.' The photos of kids with their wide smiles as they were being treated for numerous problems had drawn her in and made her rush to apply to work for the aid program. When she was told she'd be working with a gynaecologist and not the children, she wasn't unhappy. She'd still be doing what she loved best—caring for people who needed her help. Then came the notes with Fergus's name, snagging her attention the moment she'd opened the letter. Was someone playing games with her? Stirring up trouble when it wasn't necessary? If so, it was up to her—and Fergus—to keep trouble out of the picture. They both had far more important things to do than get in a pickle over something long over.

'Be aware it's hard to say no after you've done it once. The people get to you with their gratitude and stoic attitudes.'

'I'm not surprised.'

'Done lots of travelling, have you?'

The questions were endless. What was he trying to do? She wasn't about to give him her life story. They'd never been friends, just circling teens using sharp retorts to try to put each other in their place. They were complete opposites in character. *Opposites attract, don't they?* Not in this case!

'I have.' She filled her mouth with chicken and salad and chewed slowly. She'd been to a few countries, worked in some of them since her marriage fell apart four years ago, when John had blamed his affair on her. Apparently, she was cold and unloving, so he'd had to look elsewhere for pleasure. He hadn't wanted their marriage to be over, he'd assured her. Tamara was the perfect woman to be the mother of the children they had started trying for, but he'd needed some fun on the side and he'd found that with an ex-girlfriend who didn't want kids. She'd finally accepted their marriage was over and, feeling grateful for not falling pregnant to John, she'd packed up her possessions along with her broken heart and walked away. Four years of marriage to a man she'd once adored, and she had nothing to show for it except a lot of distrust and a deep fear that John was right about her not being a warm, loving woman. Sashi and Dad had vehemently disagreed and said she was the warmest person they knew. But what did they know about her intimate life? Nothing.

It had been lonely adjusting to being single again. Her dreams and hopes for a happy future with John and their children had disappeared in an instant and she'd struggled with the transition.

Returning home to nurse her father had come at a time when she'd needed a change of direction. Her biological clock had started ticking. At thirty-five she was still young enough to have a baby, but she wasn't looking for a man to love because John had already proved she couldn't trust him to love her back. Neither did she want to be in her forties when, or if, she started a family. Her sister's children would be leaving high school by then.

'Favourite place you've visited?'

Weren't there other movies he could watch if the one he'd chosen wasn't to his liking? 'Paris.' She sipped her drink. 'No, actually—Sydney.'

'So you're a city girl at heart.'

'Not always. I worked in Sydney for a year and lived in the burbs.'

He smiled. 'Burbs. Now you're speaking like an Aussie.'

That smile struck hard where she least needed it. Right behind her ribs. *Warning, Tamara! This man still cranks up the heat like crazy.* She forked up another mouthful of chicken, determined not to continue this pointless conversation. Nor to be on the receiving end of another of those devastating smiles. They were trouble, which was the last thing she needed. She was here to look out for her patients, not get tied up in complicated knots with the one man she should only want to know as a colleague. Because he really was nothing like the type of man she was usually attracted to.

Of course, she wasn't giving him a chance to show how different he was now. It was obvious he wasn't the arrogant prat she'd once labelled him. That guy wouldn't be sitting cramped in the seat beside her sounding as though he wanted to know her better. He'd have been looking down his nose at the cargo pants and plain pink T-shirt she wore. Fergus had changed and, so far, it seemed to be for the better. 'Did you go offshore when you were specialising?' A lot of Kiwi doctors did as part of their training.

He nodded. 'I went to Edinburgh. My grandmother's a Scot who came to New Zealand in her twenties,' he added as an explanation. 'I had an amazing time and was very tempted to stay, but—' He paused, staring at the back of the seat in front of him. 'My grandparents are getting on and they've done so much for me that I want to be around for them.'

Her determination to keep him at arm's length backed off some. 'Good on you.'

Fergus slid the earplug into his ear and pressed the screen in front of him. 'Thanks.'

A softness Tamara never expected to feel around Fergus slipped through her. This was definitely a different man to the one she remembered. He might've been able to turn her on with a look back then, but she'd never heard him speak with such affection about anyone before. Obviously, his grandparents meant a lot to him. She finished the bubbles and picked up her book, holding it awkwardly over the tray. Who would've thought she'd be thinking that? Were his kisses still as sensational? Nope—she definitely shouldn't be thinking *that*!

Fergus nudged her, his earplug in his hand. 'You do realise you're going to be working with me?' The earplug went back in place and the movie started again.

She nudged him back, waited until he was looking at her. 'It's fine.' She'd make sure of it for a comfortable working environment, if nothing else.

CHAPTER TWO

TAMARA HOPPED OUT of the van that they'd ridden in from the airport with Fergus at the wheel. She stared around. The hospital was single level, with hibiscus plants growing along the front wall, and lawns spread out to the sides with bushes and flowers swaying in the light breeze. 'It's lovely,' she sighed. Prettier than the photos had suggested. Hospitals weren't designed to be pretty. They usually had a severe 'this is where people help you through your pain' look.

'Our accommodation's only a couple of streets away,' Fergus said as Sarah and Tim joined them. 'I figured it wouldn't hurt to do a drive-by before going there.'

'As tempting as it is, I'm not going inside right now. Might get nabbed to help with something,' Tim said. 'Though I know that's why I'm here.'

'Tomorrow's soon enough to get started,' Tamara agreed.

'Let's sort out our rooms, then go for a wander

around town,' Sarah suggested. 'I need to stretch my legs after sitting in the plane all that time.'

'Me, too.' Tamara clambered back into the van, thinking Fergus looked disappointed that they weren't going inside the hospital. 'You can drop us off and come back,' she said to him.

'No way. Despite the information I've read and the photos online, I expected something a little bigger.'

'Does it matter?' The notes had said the local medical service was basic, hence why they were here. There were waiting lists for minor to moderate surgeries that stood little chance of being shortened without outside help.

Fergus shrugged. 'Not really. I should've known better after other places I've volunteered at. I feel for the locals, although from what I've seen, they often don't seem too worried and just go along with what's available.'

'We don't know how lucky we are at home.'

'No, Tamara, we don't.' He got into the van and turned on the engine. 'Let's do this, guys.'

Two levels above the main street, the accommodation was basic but clean and spacious. Sun pelted the windows. Tamara gasped and opened them to let in what little breeze was available before opening her bag to grab a pair of shorts to change into. 'Unreal.'

'Keep the fly screens in place.' Fergus stood in

her doorway. 'The mozzies will drive you nuts. You don't want to get malaria either. It's awful.'

She'd been vaccinated. 'You've had it?'

'Afraid so. I was vaccinated for it, but either the mozzies ignored it or the vaccine was out of date. I was in Thailand at the time.'

'Working?'

'I did one of my medical aid stints there.'

'Seems unfair you got malaria.'

He smiled. 'I agree.'

That blasted smile. She preferred he didn't look at her kindly, then she wouldn't get in a knot over him. 'What do we do about meals? I see there's a kitchen downstairs, but it doesn't look like it's been used in forever.'

'We'll mostly eat at the hospital during the day. I don't know about you and the others, but I like to eat locally for dinner.'

'Count me in. Um, what I meant was I'll probably do that too.'

'I get it, Tamara. I'll see you downstairs when you've changed into those shorts. The others will be there soon.' He was gone.

Leaving her feeling out of sorts. She'd started out thinking she'd be on edge around Fergus, and that he'd be rude and unpleasant all the time. So far that wasn't true. He was going out of his way to be friendly. How was she supposed to deal with that? *You could move on.* They didn't have to become best buddies, only needed to be civil at work and even away from it. Zipping up her denim shorts, she figured there was nothing to lose going with the friendly approach. It wasn't as though Fergus could belittle her. She was strong, knew her capabilities and got help when she wasn't managing something.

Swinging her bag over her shoulder, she locked the room and headed down to join the others. She was going to make this work. Four weeks wasn't forever, so why waste time being uptight and looking for trouble that might not exist? It would only spoil the enjoyment she planned on getting from being here.

As they wandered along the pavement where racks of clothes and other temptations for tourists stood outside shops, Fergus thought about the last volunteering trip he'd done in the Cook Islands. He'd enjoyed meeting the locals at the hospital and at the various markets he'd frequented for meals. It'd been hard to pack up and leave, but he'd needed to get back home to New Zealand. The easy lifestyle had really appealed, but he knew he'd soon tire of it and be looking for more to keep him occupied. Anyway, part of setting up the clinic with his friends was so he could settle permanently for the first time since leaving Nelson to go to Dunedin.

Keeping busy when not studying or working had been what'd got him through the years after his world had been turned upside down. His grandfather had pointed out that while he was not responsible for his father's crimes, or the life his father had given him, his future was his to sort out, no one else's. His grandparents had been there for him whenever he stumbled, as he was certain they'd have been for his father when he was growing up. He'd never found out why his father had done what he had. He came from a middle-class background, never wanted for much, and yet obviously it hadn't been enough. Had it been greed? Or a desire to be admired for being wealthy?

Even now, thinking about those months after he'd learned what had been going on and all the lies his father had told anyone who'd listen to him, Fergus shuddered with horror and remorse. Not because his life had changed so drastically and fast, although that had been shocking at the time, but because of the people who'd lost so much because of Jim Collier's actions.

Despite not knowing where the money that'd paid for his lavish lifestyle had come from, when it became clear what had been going on, he'd wanted to raid a bank and pay everyone back. He grimaced. If only it could've been that easy to rectify everything. One night before he went to trial, his father had said that if people were foolish enough to hand their money over to him, then they deserved to lose it. The next day, when Fergus had asked him if he'd meant it, his father had denied saying anything so stupid. In fact, he'd always denied all the accusations, and had until the day he'd died. Hence why Fergus had refused to have anything more to do with the man who'd sired him. If he couldn't even admit what he'd done, then he hadn't deserved his son's support.

As for his mother, it wasn't an easy relationship either. He believed she'd been so embarrassed she'd married a criminal that she couldn't face anyone she knew. On the other hand, she'd quickly found someone else; they'd been married nearly ten years now and seemed happy.

All of which made Fergus wonder about love and how anyone could really be certain they'd found it. Or how it could last through thick and thin. Caution was his middle name when it came to getting too involved with women. He'd once come close to being married, had actually believed he'd found the *one*.

He'd met Harriet at university in Dunedin and they'd hit it off straight away. She'd said his past didn't bother her one iota when he'd opened up about it, that it was Fergus she loved, not his father. When he proposed two years later, Harriet accepted. He couldn't believe how lucky he was. Until Harriet took him to Wellington to meet her parents. They recognised his family name and immediately knew who his father was. Appalled, they'd convinced Harriet that by marrying Fergus, her career in media would be badly affected, and that any children they might have would need to learn to live with what their grandfather had done. Harriet had returned the engagement ring he'd had specially made, unable to look him in the eye. He'd felt vulnerable ever since. Another mark against his father.

He'd let Harriet go without an argument. No point trying to hold on to her when he wasn't right for her. She'd further rubbed salt into his broken heart when she quickly found a new partner, who was a CEO of an international forestry company, and married him.

Once again, he'd misread the person closest to him. Harriet's desertion had hurt him as much as, if not more than, his father and his former friends had. It showed how useless he was at reading people correctly, at understanding them. He obviously couldn't see past the faces they wore to what was really going on in their heads.

There were exceptions. He knew he could love and trust his grandparents. Same went for Kelvin. But could he trust anyone else ever again? He wanted to. Big time. He knew he'd missed out on so much by protecting himself, but there were only so many knocks he could take. Nowadays his relationships were only about fun and were always short-lived. Nothing long-term in the cards for him. He was certain of that.

Light, happy laughter caught his attention. Tamara.

She stood at a stand of sunhats wearing a wide-brimmed straw hat.

Sarah held out another one. 'Try this. No pink elephants in sight.'

'Aww. I like elephants.' Tamara swapped hats, tugging her ponytail through the fastening at the back. 'What do you think?'

'Suits you,' he said instinctively, and winced. The question hadn't been directed at him.

Tamara grinned. 'You reckon?'

'He's right. It does,' Sarah agreed.

He'd said his bit; he wasn't saying any more. But— 'Go on, buy it. The shop owner's looking hopeful.'

'You've got me.' She headed inside to pay for the hat.

Watching her, he felt unusually warm. No surprise she'd put her hand in her pocket to help a local. What was a surprise was how much he still liked her, even though their relationship was touch and go at the moment. She'd always been a friendly girl ready to give a hand to anyone needing it, so nursing was right up her alley. Why hadn't he understood what that meant all those years ago? He might've been a horny teenager, but letting his ego get in the way of getting to know a girl properly, beyond a kiss or two, had caused problems with Tamara. Because there hadn't been any kisses for them. She'd made sure of it. Until the ball, when they'd both imploded with long-suppressed desire. If his so-called friends hadn't turned up when they did, who knew what they might've got up to. He badly regretted not sticking up for her. He also regretted not apologising to her at the time. Yep, definitely an egotist back then. Not so much now. Did he show Tamara that or let her think he hadn't changed? Keep her at a distance? Somehow, he felt he might need to do that if he was to get through the coming weeks without becoming drawn to her all over again.

Tamara walked out of the shop wearing the sunhat, with a wide smile lighting up her face. 'Who's next to buy something?'

A challenge if ever he'd heard one. He didn't need a sunhat. Or anything else, really. He travelled lightly. Had done since he'd left school and Nelson behind him. But he was here to support the locals.

'I'm going next door to look at T-shirts.' Tim had beaten him to it.

'Me too.' He followed the other doctor.

'We've only just arrived. At this rate we'll need extra suitcases to get everything back home.' Sarah laughed.

'There's a shop selling those too,' Tamara replied with a grin.

Turning around, Fergus sucked in the sight of her happy face and wanted to freeze it in place. She looked stunning when she relaxed. Not that she didn't look lovely any time. An image of her in that aqua-coloured, floor-length, body-hugging dress at the college ball popped up. She'd mesmerised him. No other girl had made the sparks fly as high and bright as Tamara had when he'd kissed her. Why hadn't he stood up for her and told his mates where to go? He'd hadn't forgotten the hurt in her eyes, followed by fury, before she'd told him exactly what she thought of him. It had been the first time he'd realised he wasn't a gift to all females, that they weren't all going to fall for him in a blink. Yes, he had been an egotistical know-it-all, but he'd improved. Hopefully, a lot. Over the years he'd certainly worked hard to turn himself around. Being with Tamara for the next few weeks would soon show him if he'd succeeded or not.

After strolling the length of the street before heading to the sea front with everyone carrying shopping bags, the four of them turned into a café bar and sat at a table on the covered deck overlooking the harbour. 'This is magic,' Tamara commented, looking around. To think last night she'd been staying in a hotel at Auckland Airport with a view of the terminal, and now here she was, looking out over the boats tied up to jetties and moorings with people she was just getting to know. That included Fergus. She didn't know him, not this version, anyway, and she had to admit she wouldn't mind changing that. If she could trust him to be different.

'What does everyone want to drink?' he asked.

'Beer.'

'Beer.'

'Beer.'

'Guess that's four beers then,' Fergus teased with a grin. 'I'll get these.'

'You don't have to do that,' Tamara said. 'I'll get mine.' She wasn't going to be obliged to Fergus for anything.

'I'd like to, okay?' The grin was gone, replaced by a stubborn look.

She hadn't meant to cause trouble and felt like she'd been put on the back foot. 'Thank you, Fergus. That'd be lovely.'

'Good answer.' He headed for the bar, leaving her feeling awkward with the other two obviously wondering what was going on.

Dredging up a smile, she said, 'I overreacted. Must be more tired than I realised.'

Sarah nodded. 'It wasn't a long-haul flight, but with getting up so early, along with the time changes, it does affect us. I struggle with flying no matter what the distance.'

'Not good.' She had to relax and make the most of this trip. Learn to cope with losing her dad after he'd lost his fierce battle to beat the cancer. It was hard pretending she could manage without him to talk to whenever she needed a shoulder to lean against. He'd been the best dad she could ask for, always supporting her and Sashi, no matter what. Even when he'd been grieving for Mum he'd given them both so much of himself. They'd been very lucky, and she hoped she'd been as strong and good to him in the last months of his life. She shook her head. She was deliberately getting sidetracked when she should be enjoying Sarah and Tim's company, *and* Fergus's.

'Here you go, folks.' Fergus was back, placing ice-cold bottles of beer before each of them. 'Do either of you ladies want a glass?'

Tamara shook her head. 'Not for me.'

'Me neither,' replied Sarah.

Fergus sat on the only available stool at their table, beside Tamara.

She smiled. Of course it was the only stool available. Though he could've taken it to the other end of the table, she was glad he hadn't, which didn't make a lot of sense, other than she did want to get to know him better. Who knew? She might come to like him a lot. Wouldn't that be interesting? Only hours ago at Auckland Airport, she'd been in a knot about seeing him and remembering all his awful traits, and now here she was, thinking she wanted to learn more about him. A laugh spilled out. She was bonkers.

'What's funny?' Fergus asked.

'Nothing.' Like she was telling.

'So you just laugh for the hell of it?' There was a twinkle in his eyes, so he wasn't getting uptight with her.

'Sometimes. On the good days anyway. Today is one of those.'

'What really made you decide to volunteer?'

She hesitated. How far did she go in revealing herself? Did she tell him about losing her father, the need to rediscover her mojo?

'You don't have to answer if you don't want to.'

Looking at Fergus, she saw he genuinely meant it and wasn't trying to play nice. 'I lost my father four months ago and needed to do something different to get back on track. I hope this will help towards that.'

Fergus made to lay his hand over hers, then abruptly pulled back. 'I'm sorry to hear that. It must be hard waking up every morning knowing he's gone.'

'Very.' *Stop. That's enough.*

'So that's why you're still in Nelson.' His hand wound around his bottle.

'Yes. I'd been working in Greymouth before. After Dad died, I stayed on in Nelson to be near my sister. She's got a husband, and kids too.' But old habits didn't go away. Supporting Sashi came naturally.

'You're lucky to have her.' He took a long mouthful of beer.

'I am.' She and Sashi had always been close, and were brought closer together when their mother died. They'd missed her beyond description and had remained close ever since. Being the big sister—by eighteen months—Tamara had stepped into their mother's shoes. Sashi had been comfortable with Tamara being the boss. Their father had given her space to do so while making sure she didn't get too carried away. He also kept them safe and strong and able to cope. How she missed him. There was a constant ache in her chest now. But she'd come here to get back on her feet, not dwell on her loss. Picking up her beer, she followed Fergus's example and got on with enjoying the company.

The pain in Tamara's eyes when she mentioned her father made Fergus hurt for her. They'd obviously been incredibly close. There'd been no mention of her mother. There could be any number of reasons for that, but he wasn't asking. If he'd known about her father, he wouldn't have asked why she'd come to Vanuatu, thereby causing pain to surface when she'd been relaxed. Hopefully she'd get back to enjoying herself soon. He tapped her bottle with his. 'Here's to Vanuatu and doing all we can for the people who need us.'

She tapped back, giving him a small smile. 'I agree.'

'So do we,' Tim said from the other side of the table.

Fergus swallowed. For a moment, he'd forgotten Tim and Sarah were here as well. Showed how much Tamara distracted him. 'Sounds like we're all on the same page.'

'As if we wouldn't be.' Tim grinned. 'We didn't come here for an island holiday.'

'I wonder what the resorts are like,' Tamara said. 'I understand this is quite a popular tourist destination.'

'Judging by the number of people in here, I'd say you're right.' If Vanuatu was similar to the other island nations he'd been to, the locals would rarely come to the bars and cafés. These people would be tourists or on short-term contracts for road works and the like.

Sarah stood up. 'I know it's early, but I'm getting some menus. The airplane food wasn't exactly wonderful and I'm feeling peckish. Not to mention exhausted.'

'You're always peckish,' Tim teased.

'No menu for you, then?'

'Bring me one in case I change my mind.' He laughed.

'Or I could just order the burger and chips you always have.'

These two had a great relationship. He'd known

them for a couple of years and had never seen them snap at each other. Naturally, like any couple, they'd have their moments, but nothing to suggest either one had to prove they were better than the other. Exactly the sort of relationship he'd want if he was ever game enough to try again. Which he wasn't, he reminded himself as he took a sideways glance at Tamara. Small and neat with boundless energy, she could snag his attention even when he wanted to ignore her. Odd how that was the last thing he wanted to do at the moment. They were getting along just fine, not too close, not too distant. If they kept this up, work would go well over the coming weeks. It might even help him come to terms with how Tamara still made him look at her twice when he least expected it.

She was very attractive with her long blond hair tied in that ponytail, and those aqua eyes drew him in in ways he used to ignore but wasn't rushing to do now. She was still short, barely coming up to his shoulder, which suddenly made him yearn to swing her up into his arms and hold her tight, to protect her from anything life threw her way.

'What are you ordering, Fergus?' Tim asked in a welcome interruption. What on earth had he just been thinking?

He hadn't looked at the menu. 'I'll have a burger.'

'Fish, beef or chicken?' Tim asked with a wink,

knowing damned well his thoughts were miles away. He probably had a good idea what Fergus had been thinking about too.

'Fish.' With another cold beer. He was getting far too hot, and it wasn't all to do with the tropical temperature.

CHAPTER THREE

NEXT MORNING, FERGUS DROVE them to the hospital in time for their meeting with the CEO. When they walked into reception, a crowd of staff was waiting for them.

A tall, well-built man stepped forward with his hand extended. 'Welcome to our hospital. I'm Kaikea, the CEO.' He shook hands with Fergus, Tim, and then the women. 'We are so happy to have you all here.'

Let's hope that continues, Fergus thought as he looked around. He knew from previous experience that most staff would be pleased to have the voluntary service working within their hospitals to help them catch up with a backlog of patients. But not all would feel that way, thinking their abilities were in question, which wasn't the case. 'I think I can speak for the four of us when I say we're also pleased to be here.' He glanced around and found Tamara surrounded by women in scrubs, most likely nurses she'd work alongside. She wore a wide smile, reminding him of when he'd first seen her at college, laughing and chatting with a group of girls. Immediately he'd felt interested, which, as a teenage boy, had meant pretending he hadn't noticed her. There wasn't much he'd forgotten about Tamara, though. Why? It wasn't as though he'd carried a flame for her ever since. The problems he'd faced after the ball had squashed any hope of repeating that kiss they'd shared.

Kaikea clapped loudly. 'Okay, back to work, everyone. I'm sure these people want to see where they'll be working before the first patients start arriving for their appointments.'

Sarah and Tamara headed towards Kaikea, eager to get on with what they were here for. Fergus knew that feeling. The urge to get stuck in helping the women who needed his attention to turn around their lives was strong. The resident gynaecologist had taken ill six months ago and hadn't returned from treatment in Australia, so when the volunteer's commission had called him for help, he'd been quick to come on board.

'I'll talk to you in my office first, then Aisi here can take you through to Theatre and introduce you to the anaesthetists.' Kaikea headed for a door on their left. 'Aisi is our head surgeon and runs Theatre.'

They followed Kaikea, who appeared to be in a hurry to get this over with.

'Is this how it usually goes?' Tamara asked quietly.

'It's different everywhere I've been. The one common denominator is that we're needed and not resented.'

'That's a relief. I'd hate to be working with people who didn't want us here.'

For him that wasn't always so easy. 'My biggest concern is having to get very personal with women who aren't used to male doctors prodding their anatomy.'

Tamara's eyes widened. 'That never occurred to me.'

'That's because you're a woman,' he said. 'They'll be fine with you. You might have to make things a little easier for me as we go.'

'No problem. I hope I get along with them well enough so that everything goes smoothly.'

Good answer.

'What did you expect?' she asked.

'Did I say that out loud?'

She smirked. 'You did.'

'In here.' Kaikea indicated an office large enough to hold a banquet. 'Take a seat.'

Once seated Tim said, 'I'm the general surgeon. I understand we're meeting our first patients this morning.'

'That's correct. There're offices available near the reception area for you.' Loud knocking interrupted him. 'Come in.'

A woman burst in. 'Kaikea, is the ob/gyn guy here? A girl giving birth has lost consciousness in the labour room.'

Fergus was on his feet in a flash. 'Coming.'

Tamara was right behind him. 'So am I.'

Of course she was. Go Tamara. 'Sorry, Kaikea, but this comes first.'

'No problem. Catch up when you're free. Joena, please take these people to your patient.'

'I'm a midwife,' Joena told them as they hurried along the corridor. 'Nurse Isa's with my patient, but she doesn't often work with women in childbirth.'

'Fill me in on everything,' Fergus said. 'Was the birth going normally until she lost consciousness?'

'Pretty much. Inina's seventeen and had been complaining of extreme pain for hours. I couldn't find anything out of order and put the complaints down to her age. It's not uncommon with the younger mothers.'

'Where is the pain? In the birth passage? Or the abdomen?'

'Both. I wondered if baby was the wrong way round but when I checked I found the head in the right position.' Joena pushed open a door. 'Isa, here's the doctor from New Zealand.'

Fergus nodded to the woman standing at the side of the bed watching the monitor closely.

'Hello, I'm Fergus, and this is Tamara, a nurse with our team.'

'Hello. Thank you for coming so quickly.' Isa stepped back to allow him nearer the patient. 'Inina, here's a doctor to help you.'

The girl didn't move.

Still out of it, Fergus presumed. He raised her eyelids. Definitely unconscious. Why? Syncope? Quite possibly.

On the other side of the bed Tamara was taking the girl's pulse. 'Slow.'

That went with syncope, as did the low heart rate showing on the bedside monitor. 'How long has she been unconscious?'

Joena looked at her watch. 'Nearly ten minutes.'

'It could be she's suffered a syncope. If so, she should start coming round any minute. In the meantime, I'd like to check baby's position.' He went to the end of the bed and lifted away the thin blanket covering the girl before crouching down. 'Nearly there.' He looked to Tamara. 'Any change?'

'Pulse is beginning to rise.'

He nodded. 'Good. We'll let nature take its course.' He'd be keeping a steady watch over things until baby popped out. Straightening up, he turned to Joena. 'You know about syncope?'

The worried nurse looked at her patient. 'I learned about it while training, but this is the first time I've dealt with it. I was frightened there was something terrible going on. That's why I ran to find you.'

'You did the right thing. Better to get help than not.'

'She's coming round,' Tamara said.

Inina groaned as her lower body tightened.

'Another contraction. How far apart are they?' he asked.

'Last time I checked they were just over two minutes apart,' Joena told him.

Inina gave another long groan.

'I think we can expect junior to make an appearance very shortly.' He stepped back. 'You see to the birth, Joena.' The midwife looked rattled. He suspected she needed a boost to her confidence after seeing her patient lose consciousness.

Glancing at Tamara, he saw a flicker of surprise cross her face. So she still thought he was that arrogant guy she'd known before. *Thanks a lot, Tamara. You sure know how to rub in the past.* He probably deserved it, but still. 'It's the right thing to do for both Joena and her patient,' he said rather curtly.

Tamara locked her eyes on him. 'It is. I like that you understand. Not all doctors do.'

She hadn't denied what she'd been thinking. He relaxed. 'Seems I'm not beyond surprising you.' There might be more surprises to come, hopefully even better ones.

Her eyes widened, then she smiled. A genuine smile aimed totally at him. 'Seems you could be right.'

He'd take those smiles any time. They lightened his heart and made him feel good about everything. 'Right, let's get on with delivering a baby. What a way to start our time here.'

'The best, I reckon.'

As long as nothing went wrong, he would agree with Tamara on that. 'Joena, how do you want to do this? You happy taking over the birthing?'

The midwife looked surprised, no doubt also expecting him to assume the lead. Well, they both could think again. He was no longer that guy.

'I think that's best, as Inina knows me,' Joena agreed.

'Is there someone to be with her when baby arrives?' Tamara asked.

'Her mother had to pop out but should be back soon.' Joena replaced Fergus. 'Inina, can you hear me?'

'It hurts a lot,' she murmured.

Tamara took the girl's hand in hers. 'The mothers I've been with when they had their babies told me that you forget the pain the moment you hold your baby in your arms.'

Inina's eyes widened. 'Is that true?'

'I think so. I haven't had a baby myself, but I saw a few births while I was training to become a nurse.'

Fergus watched Tamara calm the girl as easily as he'd seen a mother giving her child an ice cream when they'd been stung by a bee. The ice cream had been a huge lure, and so it seemed was Tamara's quiet confidence.

Inina tensed and cried out as a contraction gripped her.

'Push, Inina,' Joena urged.

Tamara held the girl's hands. 'Come on. You can do it. Push as hard as possible.'

Fergus felt useless. There was little to say or do except keep an eye on the screen where Inina's heart rate was being monitored. After the syncope episode, he wasn't going back to the meeting in case something went wrong. It shouldn't, but he'd been a doctor long enough to know that didn't mean it wouldn't.

Another contraction. They were coming fast now.

'Deep breaths, Inina,' Tamara said quietly. 'You're doing brilliantly.'

Her voice was soft and encouraging. He could listen to it for ages. It was new to him when it came to Tamara. But then he didn't usually obsess over women's voices. He was starting to see her quite differently in many ways. She still got fired up at him as she used to when he said something she disagreed with, but he couldn't remember her ever smiling at him so beautifully as she had earlier. A strong reason to remain aloof, he warned himself.

'You're nearly there, Inina,' the midwife told the girl.

'Do you know if it's a boy or girl?' Tamara asked.

'Boy,' gasped Inina.

'Have you got a name for him?'

'No. Ow!'

'Here we go. Push hard as you can, Inina. Baby's nearly here.'

'It hurts too much.'

Fergus watched Tamara brush Inina's hair back from her sweaty face. 'Deep breath, then push. That's it. Keep pushing, more and more. That's it. You're doing great.'

'Baby's here,' the midwife said just minutes later. 'A beautiful little boy.'

Tamara handed her a handful of wipes to clear the boy's face so he could breathe freely, then he watched her awed expression as Inina held out her arms for her son, her eyes almost popping out of her head.

'My baby,' Inina cried.

The door burst open and a woman rushed in. 'Is that my grandson? Oh, he's beautiful.' She rushed to the side of the bed and sat close to her daughter, gazing in wonder at the baby.

Time to get out of here. They weren't needed anymore. He looked to Tamara and received a nod.

'Well done, Inina. We'll see you later,' she said quietly and joined him at the door.

They walked out together, closing the new family in the small room. 'That was great,' he said.

She pinched her wrist. 'I always get goosebumps when I witness a new soul arrive in the world. It is the best part of nursing, though I usually have little to do with babies in my work.'

'It's not a field you'd choose to go into?'

'No. I'm not sure why. I like helping people get better, and usually babies arrive just fine.'

'I hate the days when they don't. Even when I've handed over responsibility to a paediatrician, I can't stop worrying about the outcome.' He was talking too much, but then why not? They had shared a good experience, so there was no reason to go on alert while chatting with Tamara.

'Is that why you chose gynaecology over obstetrics? Most specialists do both.'

'I'm trained in both but lean more towards the gynaecological side.' A lot more. 'It involves more surgical procedures and less getting up in the middle of the night to deliver a baby.' He'd gone for light-hearted, suddenly aware he had no qualms about that around Tamara. If she thought he was being flippant, then so be it.

'Why that field over any other one? You could have chosen anything.'

She thought he could be an expert in whatever

he'd chosen to do? His shoulders lifted slightly. 'How well do any of us know what's out there until we're in amongst it? I got a kick out of seeing babies come into the world, which made me realise I liked working in a positive field, though I still didn't want to be a full-time obstetrician. Cutting out fibroids or doing hysterectomies doesn't sound like fun for patients, but I'm helping them improve their quality of life, and I like that.'

Of course he'd be helping patients in any area of medicine, but something about motherhood and mothers he'd seen in his first years of training had snagged his attention and made him think about what he really wanted to qualify in. He'd initially considered cardiology, but that had been the other version of himself, who'd only wanted to be a cardiologist because they were widely thought of as the crème de la crème in the medical world, not the Fergus who was struggling to overcome his father's betrayal and find himself. Finally, he'd woken up and gone for what he'd felt was right for his new persona.

'I'm glad. It would be terrible to put all the effort required into qualifying in a field you weren't suited to.' She opened the door and stepped inside.

He followed, his head spinning and his eyes on those rounded cheeks filling Tamara's light trousers. She understood him. Not something he'd expected so soon after meeting up with her again, if at all.

Sarah looked up from a file she was reading. 'How'd it go? I presume all good or neither of you would be here.'

'As I thought, the girl had suffered a syncope episode but came round not long after we joined them,' Fergus told her. 'Then she gave birth to a lovely wee boy.'

'An absolutely beautiful boy who I wouldn't call wee, though for an islander he might be a tad on the small side.' Tamara was grinning like someone had given her a bar of chocolate. 'It's a great start to being here.'

To be followed by surgeries on women who were no longer having babies for all sorts of reasons. But he'd be relieving them of pain and discomfort, which had to be good. He pulled out a chair. 'Has Kaikea handed over his office to us for the rest of the morning?'

Tim shook his head. 'He had urgent business in town so suggested we remain here to go through files and get up to speed on what's ahead for us.'

'While you're doing that I'll go and suss out the hospital, get the idea of the general layout.' Tamara turned to him. 'Unless you need me here?'

'No, you do that. I'll make notes on each patient. You can get up to speed before we see them. While you're working with me most of the time, Tim might occasionally need your assistance too.'

'No problem. I like to be kept busy.'

No surprise. This woman used to be constantly on the go whenever he'd seen her at college events. Some guys had called her the energiser. Watching her on the netball court had been like witnessing a whirlwind tearing up leaves on the lawn. Horny teens that they were, he and his mates were often there to get a look at the girls in their tight sports shorts and T-shirts. Tamara had stood out as one of the hottest. His pants were tightening just thinking about her now. How crazy was that? Many years had passed since he'd seen her in her sports gear and he was still getting hard? Hell, he was thirty-five. Those memories shouldn't be revving him up now!

Grabbing a pile of files, he opened the top one and focused on the information in front of him. He had to shove those ridiculous thoughts away, not just for now but for the month ahead.

Isa Bule, thirty-three, large fibroid over uterus.

Focus, man. It took a little while, but finally he did.

Tamara couldn't deny the skip in her step as she walked along the corridor looking for the Theatre suite. Seeing that baby boy arrive had been awesome. Inina had looked stunned, then thrilled as she reached for her son. What would it be like to bring a child into the world? Your own child. Not that it could be anyone else's, of course. One day she was going to have a baby and raise him or her with all the love that was in her heart. One day.

She slowed down, caught by a longing so deep it frightened her. She'd been thinking about having a family quite a bit lately. Since John, she hadn't considered finding another man to love and have a family with. After John telling her she lacked sexual creativity in bed, the thought of anyone else saying the same thing had scared her, so remaining single had kept her from being hurt again. She also believed having a child on her own wouldn't be fair. She knew what it was like to grow up without her mother around, but she'd at least had seven years with her and had some wonderful memories to go on with. Hugs and kisses when she'd hurt herself, stories at bedtime, hot cocoa when she got home from school in winter, being told off for eating too many biscuits before dinner. The images were endless and had often helped her to go to sleep in the years after her mother had died. Her father had also been so loving and helpful, teaching her how to find her way through life's mishaps. Her child could not miss out on having a male role model. So, no baby for her, despite the need filling her.

'Are you Tamara or Sarah?' A young woman in scrubs stood in front of her. 'I saw you when you arrived in reception with the doctors. I'm Carrie, a nurse.'

'Hi, Carrie. I'm Tamara. I'm going to look

around and familiarise myself with Theatre and wards. Sarah's joining me shortly.'

'Let me show you where everything's kept. I work in Theatre most of the time. It's fairly straightforward.'

'You're not a local, are you?'

Carrie's fair skin and blond hair gave it away, and if Tamara had any doubt, Carrie's accent sounded Australian.

'I grew up in Darwin. I came over here for a holiday with some nursing friends and never went home again. I met and married a tourist operator who'd come over from Queensland to start up a fishing tours business. We intend returning to Oz someday, but it's been five years since we first said that, and we've got no plans to do anything about it yet.'

'Hey, if you're happy, why change anything?'

'I agree. Right, in here.' Carrie led her into a small room off to the side and handed her a set of scrubs. Once dressed, they headed into the operating room, where two operations were underway. 'I won't introduce you to anyone at the moment.'

Tamara agreed. 'They wouldn't thank us for interrupting. Show me where all the equipment's kept and where the recovery room is. Here's Sarah. Perfect timing.'

An hour later, after checking out every last detail and then learning where the wards were and which was which, Tamara and Sarah went to find the men. They were in the canteen eating sandwiches and mangos.

Fergus glanced up as she approached, his serious face in place. 'Grab yourself something to eat. We've got a busy afternoon ahead, starting shortly.'

'Yes, boss.'

His head shot up, a frown appearing. 'Tamara, I'm serious.'

'So am I,' she retorted, wondering why the mood swing. 'Are you still meeting patients to discuss procedures with them?' He had indicated that he'd be doing that earlier but something might've changed.

'Yes, there're ten on today's list.'

That was quite a few when he had to discuss with each woman what he'd be doing and what came afterwards for them. It meant a heavy Theatre schedule in the following days. From what she'd been told when being interviewed to come over here, their patients wouldn't be as prepared as those back home and everything took longer. But, 'We'll manage.' Though it wasn't up to her how he got through the list. She was here to take in the details and reassure each woman they'd be fine, along with helping Fergus in Theatre.

Fergus stared at her as though she was an alien.

'I'll do all I can to help,' she snapped.

'I know you will.' The frown intensified. 'Get

something to eat. It's been a while since breakfast.'

Many hours if her growling stomach was an indicator. When she returned to the table, the others were in deep conversation. Not wanting to interrupt and receive another frown from Fergus, she concentrated on eating.

'What's Theatre like compared to home?' Tim asked as she cut into a mango.

Since Sarah had a mouthful of sandwich, Tamara answered, 'Basic, but as far as I could see, everything you need is there. Two ops were going on and the areas were constantly being cleaned.'

'I'm going to take a look before I see my first patient,' Tim said. 'It's important to know where everything is in case something goes wrong.'

'I'm coming with you.' Fergus stood up to follow Tim out of the room.

Licking her fingers, Tamara savoured the delicious flavour of the mango and waited, suspecting Sarah had something to say about Fergus.

Pushing her plate aside, Sarah put her elbows on the table. 'You all right to work with Fergus? Or should I swap places with you tomorrow?' Straight to the point.

'I'm fine working with him.'

'Why the sudden atmosphere? He got uptight a few minutes ago and you tensed up in reaction.'

'We knew each other a long time back, but I'm

sure he's told you that.' She had no idea what he might've said to Tim and Sarah, but she doubted he'd have gone into depth about how they'd reacted around each other at college.

Sarah nodded. 'He mentioned it in passing.'

So he hadn't said a lot. She'd keep it brief too. She wasn't looking for trouble. She liked Sarah, and Tim. *And* Fergus. Despite his recent grumpiness. 'We had a falling out at college that wasn't easy to put behind us, but it's in the past and now we're working together, which is good for both of us.'

'Glad you see it that way because you're both special. Having a problem between you wouldn't be great for anyone.'

'Thanks, Sarah.' Sarah's comment made her feel better considering how little they knew each other. 'When Fergus was short with me, I wondered if something had stressed him when he was going through his patients' files.'

Sarah drained her glass of water. 'From the last time I did this, I know the first days are often stressful for the doctors. The systems are different in lots of ways to what they're used to back home, and so much relies on getting it right. The staff can be wary because they think we might put them down over any little thing. Maybe Fergus is on edge about that.' Standing up, Sarah collected her plate and glass. 'I'm joining Tim and his patients. See you later.'

Leaning back in her chair, Tamara watched Sarah leave the room. The other woman had been open and friendly but obviously didn't suffer tiffs and nonsense at work. 'Not that I can blame her.' She didn't either. Tamara downed the last of her orange juice. Now she'd caught up with Fergus and spent some time talking, eating, shopping with him and the other two, she knew she didn't want to return to thinking he was an arrogant know-it-all. He had changed. To the point she barely recognised him. Except for those good looks. They were the same, though better.

Back in Theatre she found Sarah with the men discussing details with an anaesthetist.

'Ian, this is Tamara,' Fergus said at one point. 'She's a nurse and will be working mostly with me.'

'Hello, Tamara. Saw you sussing things out in here earlier. It's very basic but everything you need is available.'

'Hello, Ian.' She nodded. 'From what I saw it all looks shipshape.'

'We're seeing our first patient in ten minutes,' Fergus told Tamara. 'Let's find our office and see what's there.'

'Sure.' *We*, as in their patient, not only his, which he'd be entitled to think as he was the doctor. 'There're two rooms near the reception area that are for the team to use.'

'Good. How are you finding things so far?'

A lot better than she'd expected. 'It's pretty basic, but everyone's eager to help us, which goes a long way to making me more comfortable.'

'There might be a bit of one-upmanship going on. It's not uncommon in most hospitals. I doubt it'll be any different here.' Fergus turned to her with a small smile. 'I try hard not to be one of those people, Tamara.'

'I'm sure you do.' Totally. From what she'd seen he was relaxed around everybody. What's more, it came naturally. 'I mean that.'

His smile widened. 'Thanks. It took some work, but I think I've made it.'

Now *her* eyes widened. Did he really say that? 'You've really changed, Fergus.'

'For the better?'

'Absolutely.' As far as she could tell, anyway.

'I'll buy you a drink for that.'

She couldn't help it. She laughed. 'You're on.' So much for considering backing out of coming here once she'd learned Fergus was on the team. It was turning out to be the best thing to happen to her in a long while. He was quite the man to tickle her interest now he wasn't all about himself She had to admit he'd always drawn her attention, but now he was waking her up in ways she'd never expected. Not only because he was a hunk. Sexy as all hell, good looking, and his smiles were decimating. Kissed like the devil. Not that she'd kissed one of those, but that night of the ball had showed her what she'd been missing out on by deliberately ignoring him.

She had worked hard to deny how he made her want him. She wasn't used to retreating from people, other than back when they were sparring with each other. Sparring? That fit perfectly with what had gone on. Some verbal jabs had been harder and hurt more than others, but they had been set on pressing each other's buttons for a reaction.

This trip was turning out to be interesting in more ways than she'd expected. She hadn't thought about her father for hours at a time, which gave her room to breathe. She'd never stop thinking about him on and off, but since his death she'd hoped to finally be able to shake the fear that she wasn't ever going to have someone special in her life again. Sashi was there for her, as were her friends, but to have someone at her side permanently would be wonderful. If he could accept her for who she was and love her back equally, a man to be partners in life with.

'These the rooms?' Fergus stopped outside an open door off the corridor and waved his hand at the row of doors.

'Yes.'

'Let's bring our first patient in and get things underway.' He held out a stack of files. 'That's the order I'm going to see them in. Everything's on computer, but they like handwritten notes here.'

'Okay.' She took a quick look through the first file to get a general idea of why the woman was here. 'Fibroids?'

'Yes. They seem to be the most prevalent cases I'll be dealing with. A downside to not having a permanent gynaecologist on site.'

'Surely that's the same for everyone you're seeing?'

'You're right. Again. Okay, let's get this show on the road. You can bring in Mrs Tari now.'

Out in reception, Tamara looked around at the expectant faces and saw a couple of nervous-looking women at one end of the long seat. 'Mrs Tari?'

Sure enough, one of the two women stood up. 'Hello.'

'Hello. I'm Tamara, and I'm a nurse. I'm pleased to meet you. I'll be with you all the time you're talking to Doctor Collier.'

'Thank you.'

'Do you have someone here who you want to come with you?'

Mrs Tari nodded to the woman who'd been sitting beside her looking just as nervous. 'Emele.'

Tamara stepped nearer to her. 'Hello, Emele. Pleased to meet you too.'

'Thank you.'

'Let's go to the room where Doctor Collier's waiting for you. If you have any questions, don't hesitate to ask. He's very kind and will explain everything so you understand.'

The women followed her in silence, Mrs Tari obviously not looking forward to being examined—possibly because the doctor was male. She'd do her best to help dispel any discomfort the lady had. After introducing Fergus, she closed the door and indicated the women should sit.

'Call me Fergus, ladies. Now, Mrs Tari, I understand you have a big fibroid on your uterus. Do you know what this is?'

'Yes. My doctor told me, and my daughter looked it up on the internet.'

Fergus smiled, though Tamara knew he'd be wishing they hadn't done that. It might've made everything appear worse and frightened them. 'I'm going to operate to remove it. Are you all right with that?'

'Yes. I want the pain gone.'

'I have to tell you that you will have some pain for a few days after the operation while everything settles down and the wound heals. You will also have light vaginal bleeding for up to two weeks afterwards as the wound repairs, then everything will come right and you'll feel so much better.'

Mrs Tari nodded. 'It will get better, then? The pain really will go away?'

'Yes.' Drawing a breath, he continued. 'I need to look at your tummy and feel the fibroid to see how big it is and exactly where it is. Tamara will help you get partially undressed and onto the bed. I'll be as quick as I can, but I have to do this examination to save time later.'

Tamara closed the curtain around Mrs Tari, and when she'd removed her trousers, she covered the patient's lower body with a sheet. 'There you go. I'll be right here if you're worried about anything.'

'You're very kind.'

'I don't like patients feeling uncomfortable. It's not good for them.' She placed a hand on the woman's arm. 'Doctor Collier will be very careful, I promise.' She was certain of that.

'Are you ready, Mrs Tari?' Fergus asked from behind the curtain.

'Yes, Doctor.'

'Right. Remember, ask anything you want. Sorry if my hands feel cold on your skin.'

Mrs Tari laughed lightly. 'In this heat?'

'It's the vinyl gloves,' Tamara told her. 'They always feel cold.' She kept chatting, asking questions about Port Vila, and within minutes Fergus was tossing the gloves in the bin.

'I've seen the X-rays and the scan you had, and now I have felt the fibroid I'm ready to make you right. We're doing this first thing tomorrow morning.'

Mrs Tari paled. 'I know.'

Tamara squeezed her arm. 'At least you won't have days to think about it. Is Emele staying with you in the ward this afternoon?'

'She is.'

'Good. You can talk your heads off and relax.'

Finally, a big smile. 'We do that all the time. We're very close.'

'Nothing like best friends, is there?' Hers were amazing, and she'd do anything for them. Tamara helped her sit up and handed over her clothes. 'I'll wait for you on the other side of the curtain and then take you to the ward where you're staying.' The women probably knew better than her where to go.

Fergus was writing up notes. 'I'll see you again before you go into Theatre,' he told Mrs Tari from behind the curtain. 'If you have any doubts, then please tell me so I can reassure you everything's going to be all right.' He sounded confident that nothing would go wrong. Nor should it, but sometimes, in rare cases, something did.

Glancing at him, she found him watching her. 'It will be,' he mouthed silently.

In this situation she didn't mind his confidence. It would help calm Mrs Tari and make

Tamara feel good about the surgery. Why, when she'd seen many operations being performed, she wasn't sure. Only that she was accepting Fergus was a good guy. Something she didn't want to change her mind about.

CHAPTER FOUR

'CLAMP THE UTERINE ARTERY,' Fergus demanded. 'We're getting some serious bleeding.'

Tamara put a clamp in place, then swabbed the site. The fibroid was massive. 'You're not removing the uterus?'

'I'd prefer to, but Mrs Tari is adamant she doesn't want that. Something to do with being a woman.' Was that a smile behind his face mask? His eyes had lit up even as he focused on the procedure.

'As long as she's not at risk of cancer, I guess it's not a problem.' She continued to swab as Fergus made more incisions, oddly aware of his long fingers holding the scalpel precisely.

'No sign of cancer, and the X-rays didn't show any growths. I'll take a sample to make certain.' He cut around the fibroid, nodding to her when more clamps were needed. His hands were steady, his moves efficient. His patient couldn't ask for a better surgeon.

Fergus was the clever guy he'd always said

he was, only this was for real. He knew what he was doing, did it carefully and competently. She was impressed. He was quite something beyond how easily he caused a sexy heatwave to roll through her.

'There, done.' Fergus placed the fibroid in the bowl she held out. 'That's heavy. No wonder she was in so much pain.'

Tamara shuddered. 'I wonder why she didn't get something done long ago.'

'She might've seen a GP, but there hasn't been a specialty surgeon to do anything about it for some time. That's why we're here to catch up on the backlog of surgeries.'

Another shudder wracked her. Wait times for procedures at home weren't perfect, but no one would have to wait for a fibroid to get this big before being removed.

Fergus said, 'Prepare needles for suturing.'

'Done.' She handed Fergus the first one. 'Here you go.' After she threaded more needles and removed clamps whenever he told her to, they were soon stepping back. 'Job done.'

'One down, three to go.'

Tamara stretched up onto her toes and rolled her head in a circle. 'It'll be a long day.' Each operation would take two hours or more. 'Then there's tomorrow.' And the rest of the week, including Saturday. Sunday was their only day off.

'You're an excellent nurse, Tamara. You did

a great job with Mrs Tari.' Was he being condescending, as though he'd thought she'd be incompetent?

Or was she overreacting? The uncertainty made her tense and annoyance instantly flared. 'Why wouldn't I? I put everything into my nursing.'

'Whoa. I was paying you a compliment, not looking for trouble.' His head flipped up and his eyes were stern above his mask.

She stared at him. To be fair, what he'd said wasn't a putdown. She'd been looking for trouble, waiting to be criticised. Which she shouldn't have. There was no reason to. 'Sorry. And thank you, Fergus.'

'Let's move on. Grab a coffee before starting the next op.' He turned to the anaesthetist. 'That all right with you, Ian?'

'Go for it. Get one of the nurses in post-op to come in on your way out. Your patient will start coming round shortly. I'll join you in a few minutes.'

Tamara headed for the bathroom to divest herself of her scrubs and gloves before washing her hands thoroughly. What an idiot she'd been. The words had spilled from her mouth without thought about what she was saying, as though she was eighteen again. As she'd been continuously telling herself since arriving here, it was time to get over herself. If she didn't, she was in danger of being worse than Fergus used to be.

At the staff station she made a pot of coffee and got out mugs. When Fergus came through, she filled a mug and handed it to him. 'I *am* sorry.'

He leaned back against the bench. 'You're having difficulty thinking I've truly changed.' It wasn't a question. He was stating a fact.

She could do honest too. 'Sometimes.' She filled another mug and sipped the hot liquid.

'I don't blame you.'

Her eyes widened. Had he really said that?

A sad smile settled over his mouth as he stared at the floor. 'I mean it. I had some harsh lessons during my last term at college, but be assured, I did learn from them.'

While she had no idea how bad it had been for Fergus and how he'd managed to get through those final weeks at college, she'd heard enough gossip to know it would've been a horrific come-down for a boy who'd once been kingpin. 'It must've been a terrible time.' Everyone had been agog with shock and gossip about Fergus, even though it was reported that he hadn't had a clue what his father was up to. 'You lost so much.'

'What's that saying? Sometimes things are sent to try us? Until it all went pear-shaped, I'd have laughed at that.' His mouth was grim.

She couldn't believe he was actually talking

about it, which rattled her to the core. He really and truly meant what he said. 'Fergus, I don't know what to say except the past is in the past, and I'm forgetting all about it and moving on.'

'Ahh, but you haven't truly forgotten any of it.' He looked her directly in the eyes. 'I'm not saying I blame you. I'm merely stating the obvious. There's not a lot I can do except carry on being who I am now.'

Sucker punch her, why not? 'Go you. I can't begin to imagine how you got through it.' She was struggling to get her head around who this guy really was now. She'd never expected him to be so open with her. Sure, he hadn't said a lot about what went on back then, but at least he had raised the subject. She did want to get to know this new version of Fergus. He piqued her interest in ways she'd hadn't experienced in ages. It could be exciting if she let him in. But… *Not happening.*

'Be glad you don't have to,' he said and drained his mug.

'I am.' After her mother died, her father had been the most important person in her life growing up, and for Fergus not to have someone like Dad at his side must've been horrendous. From the little she knew, Fergus's father had egged him on to do better and better at college, to show everyone that he could have and be anything he chose just because they were so rich. 'My sister and I were very lucky to have our father.'

Rinsing his mug, he said. 'I'm pleased for you. I mean that, Tamara.'

'Fergus.' She paused. 'I know you do.' She truly did.

'Thanks.' He nodded, drew a breath. 'One more thing I should say and it's a long time coming. I am very sorry for how I treated you at the ball. I behaved appallingly in not defending you to the other guys.'

She stared at him, her mouth drying and a tremor starting up her spine. There was a steadfastness in his expression that cut through her like a blunt knife through butter. 'You did behave badly. But I retaliated and said some pretty awful things to you too.'

'Yes, you did.' He glanced at his watch. 'Right, I'm going to get scrubbed up and see my next patient.'

'Wait. Fergus.' She tried to swallow. Failed. 'That apology wasn't necessary but thank you. I really wasn't nice to you, either.'

'The difference being I fully deserved what you said.'

Strike her down. 'It's in the past now, Fergus. All of it.'

He gave her a tight smile. 'I agree.'

'I'll be with you shortly.' *And I vow to only look forward when it comes to you.* But no further than working together. Nothing Fergus could do or say would allow her to trust another man with her dreams.

The next operation was a hysterectomy on a thirty-year-old woman with a prolapsed uterus. When they'd met her yesterday, she'd sobbed as she'd accepted there was no other way round the problem. It was impossible to put her uterus back into place permanently. Having more children wasn't to be.

Tamara put on clean scrubs, her mind still going over how open Fergus had been. Never in a million years had she thought he'd be so frank with her. If he could do it, then she would too. It didn't mean they'd become best buddies, but they could get along well enough to be relaxed around each other while they were here. How he'd managed to face up to what his father had done, let alone how much his own life must've changed, was beyond comprehension, which was impressive. She'd heard a lot of his so-called friends had deserted him just when he would've needed them most. No wonder he didn't return to Nelson after leaving university. Other than bad memories, there wouldn't have been much there for him to stay for. What about his mother? She used to come and watch Fergus play rugby, always dressed to the nines and reluctant to mix with the other parents on the sideline.

Sarah popped into the changing room, tugging her scrubs top over her head. 'How's it going?'

'I'm in my element.' Nursing made her feel right at home, as though she'd been born to do it, comfortable in her own skin.

Even if it was only day two on the job, this adventure was already working out well. Nothing to do with Fergus making her feel more alive than she had in a long while. Exciting didn't begin to explain the bubbly warmth spreading throughout her. *Careful. John used to make you feel like that too.* Her shoulders sagged. *So did Fergus, once upon a time.*

Whatever had possessed him to say that to Tamara? Talking about his father never happened. Tamara probably felt smug right about now. Though she hadn't looked or sounded that way. More stunned. Guess he could still surprise her, after all. Long may that last, because he didn't want them falling out. He'd prefer to spend time getting to know her better instead of arguing.

He'd always enjoyed winding her up because when she got angry, she'd looked as sexy as hell. But he was no longer that guy. He didn't own the world. It was embarrassing to him now that he'd once thought so. He'd turned himself around and was no longer full of hubris. More importantly, Tamara was getting to him in unprecedented ways. She was smart. She was fun. She was honest—and always had been. She lit up any room she walked into. She was hot. Small and curvy, with amazing legs and a cheeky glint in her eyes when she wasn't having a poke at him. Which might be why he'd mentioned his past. He hadn't given much away, but he'd put it out there how hard that time in his life had been for him, something he never normally talked about. Except with Harriet, and in the end that had backfired on him badly. Having lost friends who'd said much the same, he knew there was nothing to be gained.

Not even his mother knew how he'd truly felt about those years. She became focused on maintaining the lifestyle she'd come to enjoy, while he'd concentrated on getting his life back on track in a way that didn't include being supremely arrogant to people. Especially to Tamara, he realised, as he looked back on it.

Tamara. What did she really think of him? She didn't hold back on standing up for herself when she thought he was having a crack at her, like when he'd said she was a good nurse. She believed he'd been surprised she was as good as he'd said. He certainly hadn't been. One thing he'd always known about Tamara was that when she wanted something, she gave it her all and then some, and that would include being a top-notch nurse.

'Alani Leconte is waiting outside Theatre.' Ian

stood in the scrubs room doorway. 'That was a massive fibroid you removed in the previous op. Don't think I've ever seen one that big.'

'It happens when there aren't enough resources to perform much-needed surgeries, sadly.'

'So they just have to grin and bear it, eh?'

'Afraid so.' He pulled on a clean top and straightened it down to his hips. 'And on that note, let's go.'

Ian smiled. 'Lead the way.'

Walking into Theatre, Fergus's gaze went straight to Tamara busy setting out the equipment he'd need during the next operation—the hysterectomy. 'You're way ahead of me,' he said, hoping she wouldn't take that the wrong way.

'I don't want any surprises like not being able to find anything you might require.' She gave him a small smile that helped ease his concern. 'I'm still learning my way around.'

Strange how he didn't want to get on the wrong side of her when that's all they'd ever done in the past, while pretending they weren't hot for each other. That could be why he felt this way. A lot had gone down in the time between then and now for him, and he knew that Tamara had faced some difficulties of her own, losing her father recently. Everyone did in one way or another. 'Looks like you've got it covered. Do you want to bring Alani in? I'll talk to her here.'

'On it. I've given her the pre-anaesthesia medication. She doesn't appear too stressed about what's ahead, which surprises me given how upset she was yesterday.'

'You can't always tell how people feel right before surgery. Some patients are good at hiding their emotions.' He'd learned that during his first time working in Theatre as an intern. A patient, a male in his forties, had come across as completely relaxed, only to start shaking and sweating when being wheeled into Theatre despite having had a pre-anaesthesia med. He began shouting that he didn't want the op. It took a lot of time and effort to calm him down. Afterwards, he'd apologised profusely, obviously feeling terrible about his reaction.

'Have you worked with Tamara before today?' Ian was at his monitors, getting ready for Tamara to bring Alani in.

'No, I haven't.'

'Well, I got that wrong. You both seem to know what the other's doing before you even do it.'

He hadn't noticed, but now hearing Ian say it, he knew that's exactly how it had gone during the previous operation. 'Tamara's good at reading situations.' Was she like that in other circumstances, or only as a nurse? He'd keep an eye out. Darn, he thought about her a lot. Too much, really, but when she made him feel so warm and comfortable it was hard not to. Now that they'd caught up in very different circumstances, he was coming to like her a lot. Tamara had turned into a mystery he'd like to unravel.

The door to Theatre swung open and Tamara pushed a bed through with his patient on board. As they came closer, she said, 'Alani, Doctor Collier's here to talk to you.' She smiled at their patient.

'What's wrong?' Alani looked worried.

Fergus quickly stepped up, working at ignoring the fluttery sensations in his gut brought on by Tamara's smile. 'Nothing at all. This is routine protocol. I'm here to reassure you and answer any last-minute questions you might have.'

'I am already uptight. Let's get it over and done with. You answered everything I wanted to know yesterday, Doc.'

'Then as you say, let's get underway. I'll see you after the op. In the meantime, you're in Tamara's capable hands.' Rubbing it in a bit, perhaps, but too bad. He liked letting Tamara know how he felt about her work, if not her. Yet. If ever. He didn't know her very well. He frowned. She could be married with kids, although according to the volunteer service CEO, she hadn't hesitated about coming over here when asked. She might be single and staying that way. For all he knew, she could spend her time travelling and working all over the world, or she might've become a hermit who never intended moving away from Nelson. Though that one seemed far-fetched, since she was already here in Vanuatu.

'You need to move over to the operating table, Alani. Think you can do that if I hold you steady?'

'Of course.' Alani swung her legs over the side of the bed and stood up, with Tamara holding her arm. Turning around she sat on the edge of the table.

Tamara lifted her legs up. 'There you go. Lie back and we'll give you another anaesthetic through the cannula in the back of your hand to send you to sleep. Start counting to ten. See how far you get.'

'One, two, three, four, fi—' Alani was out.

Tamara wiped the spot where the cannula had leaked. 'It's a very trusting moment, isn't it?'

Fergus wasn't sure if she was talking to him or Ian, but he answered, 'Absolutely. From this moment on, the patient has no idea what we might do. We do explain it all, but it's completely out of their hands.' It still amazed him how people trusted him to open up their bodies and either remove parts or do whatever he'd gone in for and not harm them in any way. They were at his mercy, and he fully respected that. It kept him grounded.

Ian watched the monitors at the head of the OR table. 'All yours, Fergus.'

Tamara moved Alani's gown to expose her abdomen. Then she swabbed the site with antibiotic wipes and stood back, waiting for him to begin.

Picking up one of the scalpels she'd put into a stainless steel dish, he made the first incision.

'Surgery day one is over and done, and every patient seems comfortable.' Fergus stretched his arms above his head to ease the kinks from his muscles. Four surgeries had been time-consuming, not to mention tiring.

'I'm going to pop in and see them all before heading back to our accommodation for a long shower followed by a walk on the beach,' Tamara said.

'Can we join you on that walk?' Sarah called across Theatre from where she'd been assisting Tim.

'More the merrier.'

'Count me in,' Fergus said. 'Followed by a beer and dinner at one of the steak houses, maybe?'

Tim wandered across. 'Seems we have a plan.'

'How did your day go?' They hadn't talked much as whenever he was free Tim was doing a procedure and vice versa.

'Pretty straightforward. Four hernias, and a rectal procedure to remove a non-malignant growth.'

Fergus laughed. 'We call this straightforward. Mind you, I suppose airline pilots say landing a 747 is straightforward.'

Tamara was shaking her head at him. 'You're nuts. Though you're probably right.'

He shrugged. 'Let's see our patients and get the hell out of here.'

Everyone headed to the wards. Fergus and Tamara went straight to Alani, who was surrounded by four little kids and a large man. 'How're you feeling?'

'Not too bad.' She looked grey, but that wasn't unusual after two hours under anaesthesia. 'Did everything go all right, Doctor?'

'Yes. No problems at all. We'll keep you on pain meds for a while so you can move around carefully and hopefully get some sleep. Otherwise, you're already on the way to getting back to normal,' Fergus said reassuringly.

'This is my husband, Mike, and these are our four little ratbags.'

'They're gorgeous.' Tamara watched them with awe. 'Bet they keep you on your toes.'

'Oh, yes,' replied Mike. 'Most of the time it's impossible to keep up with them. They'll have me feeling old before long.' He laughed.

'You're so lucky,' said Tamara with deep longing.

At least Fergus presumed it was longing. So, she wanted a family, did she? Guess that meant she didn't have any children yet. 'They are,' he agreed, and felt an unusual sense of wonder. He visualised small versions of Tamara running around and leaping all over her as these little guys were doing with their dad, and the wonder turned to a longing of his own. For children and a wonderful woman to be their mother. And his all-time love.

Did he really want kids? Since he'd decided never to get married, children hadn't entered into the picture. If he did have another serious relationship, there were no guarantees it would work out any more than the last one had, so no kids for him. Both his parents had let him down. While his dad had showered him with gross amounts of money and bought him anything he wanted, Fergus doubted it demonstrated real paternal love; instead, it had been part of his obsession over appearing richer than everyone else. As for his mother, she'd thought more about how she was going to carry on her lifestyle than her only son's well-being.

Did any of that mean he wouldn't be a good father? Neither of his parents had been great examples of how to raise a child well. He hoped he'd do better because he'd learned the hard way how *not* to do it. Something to think about, perhaps—if he ever found the courage to risk his heart again. His gaze tracked to Tamara. No way. They'd barely begun getting to know each other, yet she kept popping into his mind like she belonged there. *No way*, he repeated silently. But since his apology, he'd found himself wondering if there was a possibility they could be more than friends.

Tamara chuckled as Alani and her husband talked about some mischief the boys had got up to yesterday. ‘And you wanted more kids.’

Alani shook her head. ‘I did, but having this surgery has made me realise how lucky we are with our boys. Not everyone gets to have a family. I’ve got nothing to complain about, really.’

‘Aww, go you.’ Tamara leaned down and gave Alani a quick hug. ‘Take it easy and try to get some sleep. I’ll pop in to see you tomorrow morning before we go into Theatre.’

‘Thanks.’ Alani looked over at Fergus. ‘Again, thank you, Doctor Collier. I appreciate that you’ve come over to Vanuatu to help me, and others.’

Her husband stood up and held out his hand to shake Fergus’s. ‘Me too, Doc.’

Fergus returned his firm grip. ‘You’re welcome.’ Making people better felt good and made him believe he was a better person for it. ‘I’ll drop by tomorrow to see how you’re doing too.’

He crossed to another bed, where his first patient of the day lay dozing. He read the chart on the end of the bed and moved on to the next woman, a lightness in his step. He had turned his life around, and it might be time to think of the future and what he could achieve outside the medical world. Nothing to do with that laughter coming from Alani’s bedside. Soft, silvery laughter that sucked him in was not going to change his mind about remaining single and safe.

The sand was warm on Tamara's feet as she strolled, sandals in hand, along the water's edge with Sarah. The guys were behind them, talking about cricket. 'I should've put on my bikini so I could go for a swim.'

'It didn't occur to me, either. Not used to doing this after work.' Sarah gazed along the beach. 'It's lovely.'

'How are you finding things here so far?' Tamara asked.

'I'm enjoying it. It's similar to working in Fiji. Everyone's so friendly that it's fun just walking down the street.'

'I'm glad I got the chance to come here.'

Fergus came up beside Tamara. 'Ladies, there's a bar overlooking the beach over there. Feel like a cold one?'

'Now that you mention it, I do.' Tamara wanted to dance on the spot. This place was magic.

'Looks like they do meals too, so this might as well be our stopping point.'

The sun had set and her stomach was saying it was way past dinner time. It would have to wait. A cold beer was first on the list! 'My shout,' she said.

Fergus shook his head. 'I owe you, remember?'

'Save that for another time.' Which meant she

expected to spend more time with him outside the hospital. Of course she would, because there were plenty of hours to fill when they wouldn't be working. But doing that with Fergus? Was that wise? Men didn't fall for her and only her, did they? They sought pleasure elsewhere too. Air trickled out of her lungs. If only she could get past what John had done, she might find the happiness she longed for. She just didn't know if she'd be able to. At the bar she ordered four beers and grabbed a couple of menus for everyone to peruse.

'Are you on holiday?' the barman asked.

'Not really. We're helping out at the hospital for a few weeks.'

'You're those guys? Welcome to Port Vila. My friend is having his hernias removed by one of you next week. He's been in pain for a long time. I'm so grateful he's getting help.'

'I'm a nurse, and since that's general surgery I'd say Tim is your friend's surgeon. He's the brown-haired man sitting at that table.' She shouldn't have said that. This guy might go racing over and make a big fuss, which she didn't think Tim would enjoy. 'We're relaxing after a busy day.'

The man winked. 'It's all right. I know how to behave.' He picked up the four bottles of beer and headed around the end of the bar.

'Hey, I haven't paid.'

'This round's on me.' He placed a bottle in front of everyone. 'Welcome to Port Vila.'

'You don't have to do that,' Tamara said.

'I want to, okay?' He headed back to the bar with a smile lighting up his face.

'Then thank you very much.' She sat down, doubting he'd heard her, and placed the menus on the table. 'The barman shouted us this round.'

Fergus nodded. 'That happens when people learn why we're here.'

'Then I'll have to keep my mouth shut.'

'And spoil their fun?'

'I suppose not.' To think it was only yesterday morning when she'd first seen Fergus at the airport and hoped they'd get through the next few weeks without ripping each other's throats out. Seemed they were doing okay so far. Most of the time, anyway.

'Sarah and I are going to a resort after we finish work on Saturday afternoon,' Tim told them. 'Figured we might as well make the most of the beautiful spots around here. We'll be back early Monday, ready for another busy week.'

'Sounds idyllic,' Tamara sighed. She wouldn't mind doing something similar, but going on her own wouldn't be much fun. 'Have you got a resort in mind?'

'Port Vila Resort. We got lucky. They had a cancellation, otherwise staying only two nights wouldn't have been possible. They target long visits. More profitable, I imagine.' Sarah smiled lovingly at Tim. 'I bet you charmed them into letting us stay for such a short time.'

'Naturally.' Tim returned her smile.

If only, thought Tamara wistfully. Since splitting up with John, she hadn't experienced anything like this closeness. But then she hadn't been out there trying to find it, had she, afraid of having it thrown back in her face again. She still had dreams of the kind of marriage she remembered her parents having: strong and loving, there for each other all the time. Her sister's marriage was similar, so if Sashi could find that, so should she. One day. But it wasn't easy to let go of the feeling that John had been right about her—that she was cold and lacked sensuality and spontaneity. Sashi disagreed, but sisters were supposed to stick up for each other, weren't they? One day, hopefully not too far in the future, she might try again. Before her hormones dried up and she had to breed puppies instead of having babies!

'What do you think you'll do on our day off?' Fergus asked.

'I've been too busy to give it any thought. I would like to see as much of the island as possible over the coming weeks. Also, I want to go kayaking and give paddle boarding a go.'

'How about we hire a motorbike and do a trip around the island? I do have a license,' he added with a grin. 'In case you're wondering.'

It wasn't the license filling her mind, but the fact he'd offered to spend the day with her. On a bike. With her arms around that sensational body. *Do it. What could go wrong?* A lot. So what? She was here to have fun when she wasn't working. But fun with Fergus? *Give him a chance. Give yourself a chance.* All right. 'Sounds like a plan.'

'That's a yes?'

She dipped her head in agreement.

Fergus looked pleased. Had it been difficult for him to suggest they spend time together? Did he have similar thoughts about something going wrong between them?

'We'll have a blast,' she promised. She'd make sure they did. Then she could at least say she'd tried.

'Been on a motorbike before?'

'A few times. I knew someone who owned one.' An unpleasant memory of John presented itself. 'He liked to shock me by going too fast. In the end, I refused to go with him at all.' Another point against her, apparently.

'Trust me, I won't be doing that.'

Funny but she did trust Fergus. This Fergus didn't appear to want to show off all he was capable of, instead seemed to prefer giving others a good time. 'Perfect.' When he didn't smile, she added, 'I believe you.'

His head dipped to one side as he watched her. 'Thanks.'

'Seems we've all got Sunday sorted.' Tim stood up. 'I'm going to order. I'm starving. Must be the warm air and working in a new place. Would everyone like fish and chips with salad? It's trevally tonight.'

Tamara's mouth watered. 'Count me in.'

'Me, too.' Fergus got to his feet. 'I'll get another round of beer.'

Sarah leaned back in her chair. 'You and Fergus seem to be getting along better now.'

'Yes, we are.'

'Was it that bad whenever it was you didn't see eye to eye?'

Not going there. 'We had some issues, but I'm not talking about them. They're over and done with now.' Fingers crossed. 'We worked well together today and outside of work we are getting along. I want it to stay that way.'

'In other words, I should mind my own business.' Sarah smiled. 'I didn't mean to sound nosey. It's just that we know Fergus a little but have never heard anything about his past.'

There was a good reason for that. 'He's very focused on the here and now, and seems happy with what he's doing.' That's all she was saying.

'You're sticking up for him. I like that.' Sarah glanced at her phone. 'I haven't heard from anyone at home yet. Do they think we've gone off the planet?'

'They're probably jealous and don't want to

hear what a wonderful time you're having.' Sashi had texted earlier to ask how it was going. Her sister had been referring to Fergus as much as Port Vila. Tamara had messaged back saying everything was working out better than expected and got a thumbs-up in reply.

'I'll take a photo of the view from here and send it to everyone. That'll really get their backs up.' Sarah grinned. 'I can be a bit of a stirrer when it suits.'

'Here you go.' Fergus placed a beer in front of her. 'The fish and chips look awesome. I saw a plate being taken across to the table at the other end of the deck and immediately my mouth watered.'

'Excellent. This is turning out to be the perfect end to a hard day at work.'

'We'll probably do this most days we're here.'

'Don't say that. I might not want to go home again.' Though the food wasn't cheap by any means. Nothing was from what she'd seen so far, but she'd been warned about that before leaving home. Lunch was provided by the hospital, as was all the coffee or tea they could drink. Other meals were theirs to sort out. As they were a volunteer team here to help because people couldn't afford the medical expenses, she wasn't complaining. It was part of the deal she'd happily signed up for.

'I asked the barman where to hire a motorbike and he's given me two numbers to call. Both mates of his, but that's fine.'

'So we're on for Sunday.' It was exciting to think about riding around the island and discovering beaches and waterfalls and resorts with dining facilities. 'Great!'

Fergus frowned. 'You really are looking forward to it?'

She sat back. 'Have you changed your mind?'

'Not at all. I just didn't expect you to be this willing.'

'You're sounding like a wet blanket, Fergus.'

He instantly looked contrite. 'I didn't mean to be. I don't know you well, that's all.'

'At least you're honest. I think we've done okay so far. We haven't lost our cool too badly with each other.'

'You're right, and it's refreshing. If I may say so,' he added in a hurry.

He seemed more worried about their past than she was, and that said a lot because she'd been in a ball of knots for days before flying over here. 'As I've already said, despite what went down between us, I'd like to think we've moved on and can at least be friends.' That came out a little abruptly, but she wasn't apologising. He needed to understand she wasn't playing games here.

'We can, and we are.' Although a little forced, his smile was devastating. He could still charm the pants off anyone he wanted to.

Her pants were still in place despite how he made her feel. But her face was heating up and sitting under the deck roof, she couldn't blame the sun. She hated to imagine what he might be thinking about that. Nothing sensible, or even inane, came to mind, except memories of how he used to tease her and make her feel hot and needy, so she took a swig of beer in an attempt to calm her brain. But damn it, he was getting to her in ways she'd never have believed possible. Not when it came to Fergus Collier.

She wasn't falling for any man. Especially not this one. Turning her back on him, she stared out over the water, seeing nothing. *Fergus, I am not letting you in.*

CHAPTER FIVE

ON SATURDAY MORNING, Tamara leapt out of bed bright and early. Despite a busy week with a heavy workload, she felt energised in ways she hadn't since her father became ill. Nursing him had been exhausting, knowing she was losing the one person who'd always been there for her and her sister throughout their lives. But today she felt alive, ready for the world and whatever it brought. Starting with a fast walk.

Throwing on shorts and a T-shirt, then walking shoes, she headed down to the beach. At six, the sun had barely risen. The beach was empty except for a couple of fishermen on the jetty. Setting a fast pace she headed for the far end.

'Tamara, wait up.'

Spinning around, she saw Fergus jogging towards her. How had she missed seeing him? Couldn't she have a quiet walk by herself? Then, noticing those long legs eating up the distance between them, she decided being alone wasn't necessary. He was good looking in every aspect.

Shut up, brain. I don't need to hear that. 'Morning, Fergus.'

He slowed to stop beside her. 'Hi. How far are you going?'

'To the end and back.' Obviously. She wasn't going to spend the day sitting at the far end.

'Want company?'

'I guess.'

'I can go in the opposite direction if you prefer.'

She shrugged to hide her mixed feelings and started walking. 'Come on. Let's do this. It's a great way to get psyched up for the day ahead.'

'You don't walk along Tahunanui Beach every morning?'

'I don't live within walking distance, whereas rolling out of bed to walk out the door almost onto the beach is perfect.'

'It does take the fun out of it when you have to find car keys, drive a distance to the beach, all the while keeping an eye on the time because you've got to get to work in rush hour.' He was laughing at her. Rush hour in Nelson was a doddle.

'Cheeky blighter.' She picked up her pace.

He stayed beside her all the way. She didn't waste breath on talking, just kept pace and looked around as she went. When she stopped at the end of the beach she rolled her shoulders. 'That feels good.'

Hands on hips, Fergus stared out to sea. 'It's a beautiful place, but most island nations are.'

'Been to many?'

He nodded. 'I've done similar work in Suva and Rarotonga.' Then he clammed up.

She decided to open up a little. It might lighten things between them further. 'Dad took my sister, Sashi, and me to Rarotonga when we were young teens. Absolutely loved it. I want to go back one day.' When she had time and one of her girlfriends was available to join her. It wasn't really somewhere to go alone.

'It's a special place.' He began walking back the way they'd come, slower this time. 'You've mentioned your dad, but not your mother.'

Hmm, true.

'Don't answer if you don't want to.'

She shrugged. There was no reason to hold back. Friends shared stuff like that, didn't they? 'It's all right. Mum died in a trucking accident when I was eight and Sashi seven. Dad raised us on his own, the best dad ever.'

'What happened? Did a truck hit her car?'

She smiled wryly because a lot of people thought that. These days she didn't get upset thinking about what had happened. There was nothing she could've done to change it. Besides, she'd learned to live without her mother a long time ago. 'The other way round. Mum was a truckie doing long haul between Nelson, the Picton ferries and Christchurch. A car crossed the median line in front of her. She tried to avoid hitting it to her detriment. The truck rolled over a steep bank. She didn't stand a chance.'

He touched her shoulder. 'How did you deal with that?'

She shook his hand away. This wasn't a moment to get all hot and tight. 'I didn't at first, but as I said, Dad was there, helping us get through it all while coping with his own grief.'

'What a man.'

'Absolutely.' That was all she was saying, nothing about the cancer and how it had felt watching her dad fade away in pain. Too soon. It had been such a horrible time. Even knowing it was impossible, all she'd wanted was to make him better. Watching his life slowly drain away and knowing he would never recover had broken her heart. He'd done all he could for her, and she'd done all she could for him. It hadn't been anywhere near enough.

Fergus glanced at her and opened his mouth to say something, then closed it again. Had he seen her anguish?

She hoped not. She didn't like to appear too vulnerable. They might be getting along, but she wasn't up to showing her feelings about a lot of things. She'd learned that when her mother died. Everyone was helpful and friendly for a while, and then they'd moved on and she'd discovered they expected her to do the same. They had a point, except it had taken her a long time. Possibly because she'd been so young. Anyway, she was here now, on this beautiful island, and was supposed to be enjoying herself, right? Why spoil the moment?

She looked at the closed cafés along the beachside. 'Too early for breakfast.' She could do with something more exciting than toast and honey at the hospital canteen.

'How about the cafe next to where we're staying? They open early.'

'Fine. I could go for eggs on toast. Along with fresh fruit. Tropical fruit here's to die for.'

'I agree. Getting it straight from the tree makes all the difference.'

'How many patients are you seeing today?'

'Four. Nothing major since we've got tomorrow off. Who knows? We might even finish early.'

'If we do, I'll go for a swim.'

'I've booked a motorbike for tomorrow. You're still on for a ride?'

'You bet.' She'd said she'd go, and wouldn't change her mind without a strong reason, which so far hadn't occurred.

'Great.'

The cafe owner was putting out the open sign as they walked up the road. 'Hello, you two. Feel like some brekkie?'

'That's our plan,' Tamara said.

'We're still getting organised but take a seat and I'll bring menus. The cook will get on to whatever you want straight away. I know you've got to get to the hospital to start work.'

'We're getting known around town,' she commented.

Fergus sat opposite and picked up a menu. 'It feels good, like we're a part of the community for a while.'

'Different to Auckland.' Large cities didn't do that.

'Completely, which was why I moved there.'

Her eyes widened. He was admitting that? Honestly he'd been admitting a lot of things over the past couple of days. 'Did it work out?'

'Yes.'

She looked at him. 'I've never seen you look so at ease.' When he'd been hamming it up as the smartest, sexiest guy around, there'd always been a tightness about him. Now he looked more relaxed, as if he'd found his true self. 'It suits you.' Oops. Picking up the menu, she studied it intensely, wishing her words back. What had come over her? Fergus was going to think she'd lost her mind and needed locking up.

'You certainly know how to surprise me, Tamara.'

Glancing over the top of the plastic-covered menu sheet, she found him watching her with something like amazement darkening his slate eyes. 'Thought I'd always done that?'

'True.' Then, 'You don't care about that night anymore?'

Maybe they couldn't fully move forward without putting some things straight. 'No, I don't.'

'Excuse me, what would you two like for breakfast?' The café owner stood by the table. 'I'm Max, by the way.'

'Tamara?' Fergus asked.

'Poached eggs on toast, please, plus a pot of tea.'

'Bacon and eggs, and a long black, and I'm Fergus.' He sat back watching her. Waiting for her to continue what she'd started?

Best to get it over with. 'Holding a grudge after all this time is pointless. When I first learned you'd be working here, I confess I thought about pulling out but then figured that was stupid. If we couldn't get along well enough to look after patients, then we shouldn't be doing what we do for work.' She sipped the water Max placed in front of her. 'A lot's happened in the intervening years. Why waste time over something that seems almost trivial now? You had a lot worse to deal with back then.' She wasn't mentioning her father again. 'How you got through, I have no idea, but you've survived and grown a lot.' Time to shut up, or the Fergus she used to know would get up and walk off.

He didn't say anything for so long she began to expect him to do exactly that. Finally, he drew a deep breath, and said quietly, 'Thank you. I have changed. It was a dreadful time, but I do wonder if it hadn't happened, would I still be an arrogant arse? Or worse.'

Not a lot wrong with his backside these days, but she wasn't saying that! 'Nothing's ever straightforward, is it?'

'You can say that again.' He held his hand up in a stop sign. 'Don't bother.'

'Spoilsport.'

'One tea and one coffee.' Max placed mugs on the table.

'Nothing like tea to start the day.'

'After a walk on the beach.' Fergus smiled, truly at ease now.

She was coming to appreciate him more and more. They were getting along just fine, and, if any hiccups arose, hopefully they'd get through them without any difficulty.

Don't let the reins go too soon, Tamara.

A loud screech sounding like metal on metal rent the air, followed by a loud bang as though something had hit the floor in the direction of the kitchen. A scream sent a shiver down Fergus's back.

'What the hell?' He leapt to his feet, quickly

followed by Tamara, who headed towards the door the staff used.

'Sounded like it came from through here.' She carefully opened the door, looking behind it before going all the way.

Over her shoulder Fergus saw a man sprawled on the floor between a bench and the ovens. 'Hey, mate, what happened?'

'Tyler was prepping steak and slipped over. Had a knife in his hand,' Max called from the other side of the kitchen. 'Don't know where that went.'

By the look of it, into his upper body, if the blood beginning to stain his white apron was any indication. 'I'm going to check him over, all right?' Too bad if Max said no, he'd do it anyway.

'Go for it, man. Glad you're here.' Max had come around to stand at Tyler's feet. 'I'm not good at this stuff.'

'Not many people are,' Tamara said as she knelt down beside Fergus. 'Roll him over, do you think?'

'Only way to get a look at what's going on. I'll take his upper body while you move his hips and legs.' It wasn't going to be easy in the narrow space but essential if they were to help Tyler.

Max knelt down. 'I'll shift his legs when you tell me to.'

'Thanks.' That'd make things easier for Tamara. He put his hands on Tyler's shoulders.

'Tyler, this might hurt, but we have to get you on your back, okay?'

Something sounding like *yeah* came from the guy.

'Right, you two ready?'

'Yes,' Tamara and Max answered.

'On the count of three, turn him towards Tamara.' He drew a breath, aware they knew nothing about what they'd find. It could be a nick in the skin or a serious internal injury. 'One, two, three.'

Tyler groaned as they eased him onto his back. The knife was embedded below his ribs, blood seeping out slowly. Removing the blade could exacerbate the bleeding. Best leave it where it was until they got Tyler to hospital.

'His breathing's rapid,' Tamara pointed out.

Due to a pierced lung or shock? 'Max, call the ambulance. Tell them it's urgent. Then grab your first aid kit if you have one.'

'Sure do.' His phone was already in his hand and he was punching in the emergency number while moving towards a cupboard at the back of the kitchen.

Fergus had seen Tyler wince when he mentioned this being urgent. 'Tyler, we're being cautious here until we find out what injuries you've sustained.'

'Okay.'

'Did you bang your head on the floor when you fell?'

'I think so. Slipped on something.'

'Looks like oil to me,' Tamara noted. 'There's a skid mark near his feet. We need to watch out for that.'

Another man in an apron appeared at the end of the bench. 'I'll clean it up now. I was outside in the chiller and didn't know anything happened. Is Tyler all right?'

Gently pressing around the area where the knife was, Fergus couldn't feel anything to gain any more knowledge, but he kept pressure on the area to slow the bleeding. 'Too soon to say.' Bowel damage or a punctured rib were on the cards. 'Tamara, can you keep pressure around the entry site while I check Tyler's head for injuries?'

'Sure. Pulse is slightly elevated,' she told him. 'I hear a siren. Thank goodness the hospital is close by.'

'Yes. I want to wait until we're in the emergency department before dealing to that knife injury.' The blood loss could increase drastically if he moved the knife even a little. His finger found a soft spot above the right eye. 'You landed face forward, Tyler?' He figured that was the case given where the knife went in but could be wrong.

'Yeah,' Tyler whispered. 'Feel dizzy.'

'You've taken quite a knock to the head which is why you feel like that. How's that wound, Tamara?'

'The pressure I'm applying has slowed the bleeding. Think I should remain doing this on the way to hospital?'

'I do. It'll be awkward getting you into the ambulance at the same time, but if at all possible, you should stick with it.' At least she was small, unlike him, and with everyone working carefully they'd hopefully manage to get Tyler and Tamara inside the vehicle unscathed. Then they'd have to reverse the move once they reached the hospital.

'Through here,' he heard Max saying. 'There's a doctor and a nurse with him.'

Two men in uniforms came through the door carrying a stretcher and a medical kit. Fergus shuffled sideways, remaining on his knees as he explained the little he knew about the injury. 'The sooner we get him to hospital, the sooner we can do something about the bleeding.'

The older of the paramedics nodded. 'That's best. Staying here and checking everything you say you've done is wasting important time.'

'Tamara's keeping pressure around the knife wound. Do you think we can move Tyler without her having to remove her hands?' It wasn't his place to tell these guys what to do, but he could put the idea out there.

'We'll find a way.'

And they did. Once Tyler was moved onto the stretcher, Fergus and one paramedic carried him outside with Tamara walking carefully beside the stretcher, her hands firmly in place. Taking slow steps, she got inside the ambulance with Tyler and knelt on the floor beside him, continuing to focus on what she was doing.

Fergus joined her and the senior paramedic for the slow trip to the hospital, where he went to find the HOD and explain the case, before handing over after the paramedic agreed Fergus had it in the bag.

Ten minutes later, a nurse replaced Tamara and she joined him. 'I hope he's going to be okay. It was one of those odd accidents that I can't quite get my head around.'

'Did you hear Max as we were carrying the stretcher out of the building? He was tearing into the staff over who'd spilled the oil. I wouldn't like to be the guilty one.'

'Can't blame him. It could've been a lot worse.'

'Don't say that until we know how serious the injuries are.' He didn't like tempting fate.

It wasn't until the head of the ED came to tell him Tyler needed surgery for a small cut in his bowel but otherwise would be fine that he finally relaxed. It never mattered how much he put into looking out for a patient; he never stopped worrying until it was all over.

* * *

Later that day, Tamara changed out of her scrubs for the last time and grabbed a quick shower in the women's bathroom. Saturday's roster had been tight after starting late because of helping with Tyler's operation, since there'd been a shortage of staff that early in the day. Now she was looking forward to her day off tomorrow.

As long as she and Fergus didn't get snippy at each other it should be fun riding around the island on the back of a motorbike. She shivered. Holding on to that gorgeous body was not a good idea when they were still feeling uncertain around each other, especially since he excited her too much at times. Losing control of her careful side and letting rip with what her hormones were demanding—hot, satisfying sex—would not be right, though it might be awesome to finally have sex with the guy she'd always had a thing for. Like finally laying to rest the intense desire he'd always lit within her without a single touch. Those feelings of need for him hadn't gone away. Instead, they were raising their heads faster and stronger than ever. If she didn't want to see where this went, then she needed to tell him she'd changed her mind about the motorcycle trip and she'd go paddleboarding by herself instead.

Coward.

That was one thing she could honestly say she wasn't. She always stood up to whatever was thrown at her. Except when it came to handing over her trust. When she walked out of the bathroom, Fergus was coming out of the men's room looking good in denim shorts and a white T-shirt. Her mouth watered. He was extraordinarily gorgeous. She couldn't—wouldn't—deny it. 'Hey, there.'

'Want to grab a beer and a bite to eat?'

Was that wise when they'd already be spending the whole day together tomorrow? A distraction, remember? 'Sure. I'm planning on an early night, though.'

'You having doubts?'

Her hair flicked around her shoulders as she shook her head. 'About what?'

'Tomorrow.'

He read her far too well. 'No.'

'Good. Sarah and Tim have already left on their trip. Tim couldn't wait to get away.'

'Sarah was pretty excited too. Time alone with Tim, not having to think about work is apparently the perfect break.' Hopefully riding on the back of a motorbike would be just as relaxing for her. Outside, the heat slammed into her. 'Whoa. That's the hottest we've had so far.'

'There's rain on the horizon. Could be why it's so hot and humid.' Fergus grabbed her arm and tugged her out of the way of two youngsters on skateboards racing towards them. 'Watch out, guys.'

The young boys dodged around them, one bumping her as he went.

Tamara shook herself and straightened up. 'That was close.'

'You all right?' Fergus looked her up and down.

'All good. He banged my hip, but I'd probably have been flattened if you hadn't grabbed me.' Her skin was cooling where his hand had heated her up, in complete opposite to the rest of her body as the humidity took hold.

'Boys will be boys. Come on. I could do with a cold drink right about now.' He tossed the van keys up in the air and caught them again.

'Me too.'

Fergus parked outside their accommodation building. 'Might as well walk.'

'Fine with me.'

He glanced at her. 'You're very obliging.'

'You don't expect that?' She winked to show no hard feelings.

'It's another side to you that I've never been familiar with.' He smiled.

Which got to her because it made him look way too open and friendly and adorable. She wasn't used to feeling like this about Fergus. Except she had once, hadn't she? Now the need for him was getting stronger, overtaking her reticence about getting too deeply involved with him. Some of the feelings Fergus evoked in her now felt far too similar to how she'd felt back when she was a teen and he'd teased her with that wide grin and fiery eyes, except now there was a growing, deeper sense of longing for him. 'We've never spent time together on our own. I like it.'

'You think we might've got on better in college if we'd taken time out to talk to each other without looking for reasons to cause trouble?' His smile dimmed.

Time to get back on track. She didn't want any tension between them. 'We'll never know, will we? All I can say is that it's good getting to know you now.' Leave it at that. 'Shall we go over there?' She pointed to the Port V Bar and Grill on the other side of the road.

'Might as well. Looks like half the island's come to town. Just as well I made a booking.'

'You thought ahead while at work?' He must have really wanted to spend the evening with her.

'Kaikea warned me it would be busy.'

Hopefully her shorts and T-shirt were smart enough for what felt a little like a date. No doubt she was deluding herself, but there was no harm in thinking that as long as Fergus didn't know. Was she desperate or what? Her dating life was non-existent. Her father used to tell her all the time to get out and have some fun after her divorce. She'd stuck to hanging out with Sashi and friends. So her reactions to Fergus were surprising. The desire and wonder she'd known around him all those years ago couldn't have been lying dormant, waiting for him to come back into her life. That'd be crazy. But true, perhaps? She huffed out a breath. What was going on in her head and her heart? No, not her heart. *Sure about that?* an annoying little voice asked.

Fergus nudged her. 'You still with me?'

Very much so. 'Yes.' Too much.

Walking into the bar, she was relieved to see she didn't stand out for wearing shorts. Since when did she worry about what to wear? Another new experience. Surely it had nothing to do with the company she was keeping? He looked good enough to eat, and he was dressed casually. See? They were a team. A sigh escaped. Not once during the days she'd prepared to come over to Vanuatu had she ever believed they'd become a team. Not even in the hospital, since Fergus was the specialist and therefore her boss. Proved how wrong she'd been. Again. They were good together, most of the time.

'You want the usual?'

No, tonight was different somehow. 'I'll have a chardonnay, thanks.'

'No problem.'

While Fergus headed to the bar, Tamara wandered onto the deck to gaze along the street at the shops. One was an outdoor clothing shop with racks of T-shirts and shorts with touristy logos printed on them. She'd make a note to go there to buy a few tops and shorts before going home. It was summer back home, and she was short on outdoor clothes.

'Here you go.' Fergus held out a glass. 'That's our table in the corner.'

'Cheers.' She followed him across the crowded deck. 'Are you sure they don't mind us sitting here? Someone else could use it before us.' Though she didn't want to be here all night.

'It's ours for the evening.'

She tried the wine. 'Not bad.'

'It should be good. It comes from New Zealand.'

She laughed. How could she not? Fergus looked so relaxed she felt totally comfortable. 'You're being loyal.'

'Only way to be.'

They sat for a while saying nothing, enjoying the atmosphere and warmth as they watched people wandering up and down the footpaths and stopping at shops. Sipping the wine, Tamara thought about coming here for a holiday. She'd need someone to come with her, and for once asking a girlfriend along didn't hold the usual appeal. It was being with Fergus that made her relaxed and happy. Yes, happy. With Fergus. Not that she was thinking of anything more involved than sharing a meal and being tourists tomorrow. That was enough. She still wasn't looking for anything deeper. Except the ticking baby-clock was getting louder all the time. Glancing at Fergus, her heart squeezed. Imagine little boys who looked like him? *Stop it, Tamara. You're way out of line.*

They would never get together. Fergus had the potential to hold her heart so tight that if she didn't measure up to his needs, the pain of losing him would be huge. Something she didn't want to go through ever again.

Fergus leaned back in his seat, watching Tamara while trying not to stare at her. He didn't want to rattle her, but he enjoyed taking in the sight before him. He'd always thought she was a looker, and these days she went beyond that. She was stunning and gorgeous, and made him heat up in places he needed to control.

This was not how he'd believed working with Tamara would go. He'd supposed they'd be focused on patients so they wouldn't have to try too hard to get along. He'd stopped recalling her words from that night at the ball. Instead, every time he was with her now, he wondered how he could've been so awful to her. These days, if she or anyone else uttered those words to him, he'd stop and take note, think about it and see if there was some truth in what they'd said.

He had changed. He was beginning to think that even more so than he'd once believed. Throw in how Tamara now calmly approached situations and there was a high chance they could go back to New Zealand on good terms. They probably wouldn't keep in touch, but at least the past would be well and truly buried, something he'd wanted for a long time but had kept away from doing anything about, because the first thing he saw in the faces of people from the past was the disdain that his father was a criminal. The next was the suspicion that he'd done well out of his father's ill-gotten gains and therefore wasn't to be trusted.

That really hurt when he'd put so much effort into turning himself around and not being the arrogant prat he'd once been. But he couldn't blame people for their reactions. Two of his classmates had had grandparents who'd lost money in the scam, and they'd never forgiven him for being his father's son.

Tamara wasn't holding his previous arrogance against him. He didn't know what that meant in terms of being friends, but he wasn't jumping in expecting much more to come of this time than where they were at now. Hopefully, tomorrow would be all fun and no difficulties.

About tomorrow. 'Tamara, I've changed the motorbike to a four-wheeler. I figured it would get too hot wearing protective jackets and trousers. What do you think?' He was also preventing her from wrapping her arms around him and holding on throughout the day as they rode around the island. Truthfully, he had wanted that so much that he'd decided to make sure it couldn't happen. Hard to fathom why he'd been looking forward to having Tamara so close. He wasn't open to the risk of showing his feelings—even to himself, hence changing the bike to a four-wheeler.

'I haven't been on one before,' Tamara replied.

'It's different to the two-wheeler, but I hope you'll like it. Are there any places in particular you'd like to see, or shall we take it as it comes, stopping off anywhere that interests us?'

'I like that idea best. I'm going to pack my bikini in case we come to a spot where I can get in the water. I've heard it's possible at some waterfalls.'

Tamara in a bikini would play havoc with his mind as much as her arms around his waist on the bike would have. Maybe she'd wear a bathing suit that came down to her knees and elbows. It was hard not to laugh at his own ridiculousness, but if he did, she'd want to know what was funny. He laughed anyway. He couldn't help himself. Showed how much she stirred him up.

One of those neatly plucked eyebrows rose. 'What's so funny?'

He shrugged exaggeratedly. 'You and I going for a bike ride. Who'd have thought?' Tempting her to change her mind?

'It's a bit odd, I suppose, but I'm not bothered.'

'Me neither.' The hell he wasn't. He downed

the last of his beer to moisten his mouth. 'Want another wine?'

She gave him a bewildered look. 'I've hardly started this one.'

'I could line them up for you,' he said, trying to cover his confusion. He was losing the plot here. 'I'm getting another beer, so I'll grab some menus while I'm at it.'

Tamara's face tightened. She was starting to look annoyed with him.

'You did say you wanted an early night.'

'I did.'

'Then what's the problem?'

'I'm not rushing my wine.' She wasn't messing around with playing nice, instead getting straight to the point. Nothing new there.

'I didn't mean it to sound like that.' She always seemed to have him on the back foot!

'Okay.' She sipped her drink slowly. Rubbing her point in?

He waited, sure there was more to come.

Finally, 'We're doing better than I expected.'

That was it? Understanding Tamara didn't come easy. 'We are. I'll tell you something for nothing. I'm pleased that we are. It's a surprise and yet it's not, if you know what I mean.' He wasn't sure he did, but he had to get it out there so she might understand him better.

'I get what you're saying, but occasionally I

admit I can still get a little edgy. Which is plain silly after all the time that's gone by.'

'Can't be helped. We were pretty horrible to each other.' He held up his hand. 'I'm not suggesting we have another heart-to-heart about it, only saying we've both moved on with our lives and it would be petty to drag everything up again now.'

The stiffness in her shoulders melted away and a smile appeared on her lovely mouth. 'Agreed.' She raised her glass to him. 'To friends.'

Friends was good, but despite that edgy moment the feelings filling him went beyond friendship. Something to keep to himself. He tapped his empty bottle against her glass. 'Friends.'

Taking another sip, she smiled tentatively.

More like sucker punched him. He grinned, hoping to give her the same thump in the belly as he knew his smiles used to.

She gulped.

Yes! He wanted to cheer. With difficulty he refrained and leaned back in the chair to savour the moment. Who knew what lay ahead? Finding out could be fun.

Tamara fought the urge to grab Fergus's hand and swing their arms between them as they strolled back to the apartment block. The steak and chips had been yummy, as had the cheesecake she'd finished with. As for the company, she couldn't have wished for better.

Fergus had interesting stories to tell about training to become a doctor. He hadn't spent all the time talking about himself, though. He'd wanted to know more about her. They'd discussed places they'd travelled to and found they loved Europe and hoped to visit other destinations. After getting over that brief hitch, it had turned out to be a better evening than expected. Then tomorrow they were off to explore the island.

She couldn't wait. 'Are you checking on your patients before we head out in the morning?'

'Yes, I'll drop in early to see how they're doing, so we won't be late leaving to pick up the bike and get on the road.'

'That rain didn't eventuate. I hope it's not waiting to dump on us tomorrow. Not that it would put me off going,' she added.

'Glad to hear it.' Fergus laughed. 'I'm going no matter what, and I'd like some company.'

'You're stuck with me.'

'Good.'

She wouldn't think too much about what he might mean by that, would instead take it as an indicator they were still on track to being friends. It was the easy way out; not her usual style, but with Fergus, she was finding it hard to stand up to him just for the sake of it.

'What does your sister do for a living?'

His question came out of the blue, knocking back some of the relaxed feeling. She didn't want to talk about family or personal matters. She preferred enjoying the moment, but ignoring him would create tension between them. 'Sashi's a beauty therapist when she's not busy with her kids. Who I adore,' she added for no reason. She was missing them heaps. 'They're full of mischief and love playing pranks on me.'

'Bet you give back as good as you get.'

She blinked. 'It's what crazy aunties do.'

'You're lucky to have them.' There was a wistful undercurrent to his words.

She remembered that Fergus was an only child. 'I'm very lucky.' With a bit of luck, one day she'd sort herself out and add to the family brood. Staring straight ahead, she fought the urge to look at Fergus and picture once again the little boys she'd imagined earlier.

'Not all families are close.' The wistfulness remained.

She'd like to ask about his mother but didn't want to spoil the comfortable feeling between them. 'That's what families should be about.'

'How true.' Suddenly Fergus spun around to face the way they'd come. 'Come on. I need to get back to my room and sort out a few things before we head out tomorrow.'

In other words, he was changing the subject. Fair enough. It could get intense discussing families. He was probably worried she might raise the subject of his father. He needn't. She had no intention of doing so. There was nothing to be gained by talking about Jim Collier. 'Hopefully, I'll get a decent night's sleep. The humidity makes me sweat a lot and keeps me awake.'

'Is this something that's only started since you arrived here?' Doctor to the forefront?

'Yes, Fergus, it is.'

'Glad to hear it. Can't have my nurse getting sick.'

She laughed.

CHAPTER SIX

SO MUCH FOR SLEEPING.

Tamara groaned as she rolled over in bed yet again, hours later. No blaming it on the humidity this time, either. This was a different heat, engendered by pictures of Fergus walking beside her on the beach, those long legs eating up the distance so comfortably. They'd made her feel even shorter. She barely came up to his shoulder as it was.

Her phone buzzed.

Fergus. Are you awake? the message read.

The time was five fifty. The sun must be creeping over the horizon. Yes. Had a bad night.

Shall we have breakfast here then get on the road?

He was keen. Hadn't he slept either? Was she getting to him as much as he was her? She grinned. See you shortly.

Leaping out of bed, she had a quick shower to

wash away the sweat and threw on shorts and a T-shirt. After putting her wallet and a light jersey in a small backpack, she locked her room and went downstairs to the tiny kitchen.

The aroma of coffee filled the air. 'That smells good.'

'You want some?' Fergus asked.

'No, I'll stick to my usual tea.' Coffee would have her wanting to get off the bike for a trip behind the bushes.

'Toast's on.'

'You are organised.'

'I always am.' From what she'd seen while working with him this past week, she knew that to be true. 'It saves a lot of hassles later.'

While she often left things to chance. Not the serious things, but still, she wasn't always thinking ahead about what could go wrong. 'I suppose it does.'

The toaster popped and she took a piece. 'What time does the bike rental office open?'

'The bike's been left outside the office with the keys in the letterbox. I made sure they were there before texting you.'

'Sounds like you had as little sleep as me.'

'It *was* hot last night.'

'Yes.' Did that mean he'd been in a bit of a turmoil about taking her out today, or had something else got to him? She wasn't asking. He likely wouldn't tell her. Anyway, if it had anything to do with her, she didn't want to know. Better grab her swimming gear. A vision of Fergus in speedos whammed her in the head. He'd more likely wear swimming shorts, but she couldn't see past the thought of a tight brief-style suit outlining his male parts all too well. She groaned.

'You all right?' He looked concerned.

Not at all. 'I'm fine.' After using a teaspoon to squeeze the teabag, she tossed it in the bin. She'd better be, or this was going to be the day from hell. How could Fergus do this to her so easily? She'd once despised him—even when she had the hots for him, which was why she'd spurned him, not wanting to be yet another name on the long list of girls who gave him whatever he wanted—and here he was now, walking all over her determination to remain no more than friends as though there was nothing that could stop him.

He watched her like he didn't believe her. 'It's not too late to change your mind about coming with me.'

Coming with him? Heat swamped her face. Don't go there. 'Why wouldn't I?' she snapped in embarrassment.

'Because you suddenly seem uneasy.'

'Well, I'm not.' Picking up her tea, she said, 'I'm going to add a couple of things to my bag, then I'll be ready whenever you are.' She was suddenly feeling rather scratchy. She paused, oddly unsure of herself. Something else to blame on Fergus? She turned back to him. 'I'm sorry. I'm being a grump, but I promise you I'm looking forward to going around the island. If you'll still take me.'

'Absolutely. I was probably looking for trouble when it wasn't there.'

Make her feel worse, why didn't he? He really was a great guy, nothing like he used to be, and she needed to remember that at all times and stop judging him. 'Come on, let's go have a great day.'

'You're on. But I still have to check in on my patients first.'

'I'll come and say hello to them too.'

His smile softened her insides completely. Truly a great man. One she could get to more than like if she risked dropping her barriers and took a chance.

Fergus held his breath as Tamara climbed onto the bike behind him. This wasn't going to be easy. Over the day, she was bound to bump against him, and that was going to heat him up hard and fast. Even the helmet she'd put on did nothing to dampen the attraction he felt to her lovely face.

'Ready,' she said beside his ear.

His hands tightened on the handlebars as a rose-tinged scent teased his nostrils. Man, why had he suggested doing this? 'Hold on to the side bars whenever we go round corners or over rough patches.'

'Yes, boss.'

'If only,' he muttered. At the moment, he didn't feel in control of anything, especially with Tamara ramping up his hormones like he was a teenager again. The one she refused to acknowledge, remember? Could be good for both of them if she thought he hadn't changed because then she wouldn't want a bar of him. Except he wasn't that guy anymore. 'Here we go.'

Pulling out onto the road, he headed towards the coast and the first of the stops he'd looked up online. There were waterfalls along the way where people swam and dived in the deep blue, crystal clear water. He'd need to take a dip to cool off as soon as they got there. The way his skin was on fire, the water would no doubt start boiling fast.

He sensed Tamara sitting back and looking around at the trees and thick greenery on the sides of the road. Glancing over his shoulder, he said loudly, 'It's magical, isn't it?'

She leaned close. 'Absolutely beautiful. I can't wait to see everything.'

What the heck? If he was going to spend the day with Tamara this close to him, he might as well make the most of it. He breathed deep, drawing in her rose scent again. 'The first waterfall's not far. Ready for a swim?'

'It's a bit early.'

Damn. He'd hoped she'd say she was ready to

leap in the moment she got off the bike. He could set the precedent and perhaps she'd follow. 'No such thing.'

'After you, then.'

Perfect answer.

When they arrived, he could see the sun hadn't reached the waterfall yet, but they were in Vanuatu and cold weather didn't exist. He kicked off his sneakers, stripped away his shirt, and jogged to the water's edge. Unsure how deep it would be, he held back from taking a flying leap and waded in. The level quickly reached his waist and he dived deep.

Pleasure filled him. It was wonderful being with Tamara. Popping up, he saw her coming towards him, the water covering her knees as she tiptoed over the rocky bottom. For the first time ever, he saw her body. Dressed in a lime-green bikini that highlighted her gorgeous shape and full breasts to perfection, she was all he had ever imagined and more. His chest tightened and he felt humbled. She was so lovely his head spun with a longing to get closer to her, and not only sexually.

'The water's very clear. I can see my toes.' She giggled like a six-year-old.

'Jump in. It's not as chilly as we expected.' He doubted he'd ever feel cold when Tamara was around.

Slowly sinking down she let the water come up

to her breasts and then her neck before spreading her legs out as far as they could reach. 'Wow.'

Yes, wow. But he wasn't thinking about the water.

Leaning back, he tilted his head to stare up at the top of the waterfall where the sun's rays were sparkling on the edge. A dream moment. A simple pleasure, no one else about, and nothing pretentious about the area. No huts or parked caravans nearby. Again, he used his word of the day. Perfect.

He'd come a long way from the lad who went on holidays to swanky tourist towns with his parents and believed he was in an idyllic place with everything he wanted on hand. Now he knew something like this spot was far more special. Less was more. Except when it came to Tamara. There was a lot to her, and getting to know her properly was like unravelling many layers of wrapping paper with a surprise in each one.

'I could stay here all day.' Tamara laughed. 'Except I didn't bring any food.'

'There are other days for that, if you don't fall in love with the next place we stop at.' He knew what she meant. Lying on his back, he let the flow slowly take him further down the river, soaking up the view of the bush, and the bright blue sky above. Sometimes life was indescribably good.

Scrambling to his feet, he was surprised how

far along he'd floated. Tamara was back in the same place, splashing around and ducking under the water. She appeared happy. Another reason to feel content.

Making his way back to her, he wondered if he'd ever feel this relaxed about falling in love and having the family he'd like. The idea of kids had always scared him. If he hadn't had his grandparents to look out for him in that horrific year, then he wouldn't have a clue how to be a good father. Other than be the complete opposite to his own Even then, knowing how people could taunt his kids about their criminal grandfather, it wouldn't be right to place that burden on innocent children, would it? Finding the right woman who'd stick by his side would be difficult, too, if not impossible, so he'd given up looking. He'd loved Harriet and had thought himself heartbroken when she'd left him, but now he wondered if he'd deliberately made himself believe she was exactly what he'd hoped for simply because he'd desperately wanted to be loved unconditionally.

His gaze drifted to Tamara. She was bringing far too many emotions to the surface that he'd thought long buried. She'd always got his attention but now appeared to be doing so in lots of ways he hadn't thought possible. Was he open to that? To letting her in? He couldn't be sure, and he wasn't prepared to think about that now, scary as it was. Wading through the water, he joined her.

'Thought you'd gone to sleep at one point.' Tamara laughed.

'It wouldn't have been hard to. It's wonderful lying back and letting the current take over. You should try it.'

'No, thanks. I like knowing where I am at all times.'

What would it take to distract her from focusing too hard on what she was doing? 'Shall we move on to our next destination?'

'Got something in mind?'

'There's a place where you can go zip-lining down the hillside. We should give that a crack.' Would that be pressing her worry buttons? She'd know where she was but wouldn't be able to do a thing about controlling the ride.

Her face lit up. 'You're on.'

'I really don't know you. I expected you to do a runner at the thought of flying down a wire.' Then again, Tamara didn't tend to run away from difficulties, did she?

She laughed.

A deep laugh that made his knees knock.

'That is so not me.'

He swung her pack over his shoulder. 'Let's get back on the bike.' Then he had an idea. 'Do you want to take the controls?'

'I wouldn't know where to start. Anyway, I'm

happy being the passenger and gazing around at everything we pass.'

'I could be your instructor if you change your mind.'

Her sodden ponytail slipped back and forth over the back of her neck. 'Not likely. I prefer to sit back and enjoy the day.'

Fine with him. Enjoyment seemed to be the new word of the day. Long may that continue. Pulling on his shirt, he straddled the bike and waited until Tamara was seated behind him, then booted the accelerator. They were off to the next adventure. This time in the jungle.

Tamara held the zip line bar tight and waited to go whizzing down towards the bottom of the cliff face. It wasn't too steep. She couldn't wait to get started.

'Make every moment count,' the guide said. 'Your ride will be over almost before you've started.'

'Bring it on.' Looking around she found Fergus on the ride behind her, looking as excited as she was. Giving him the thumbs-up, she faced forward again.

'Ready, steady, go.' The guide released the harness holder and she was off, zooming down the cable towards the trees at the bottom. Air whooshed past her face and her hair flew behind her. 'Yahoo,' she yelled as everything sped by in a blur. Then she was rushing up to the platform, slowing as the pulley rose to where two men waited to catch her. 'That was amazing,' she babbled as they undid the harness for her to step out of. 'Thank you, guys. I loved it,' she said as she high-fived both of them.

Stepping aside, her body fizzing with excitement, she watched Fergus come flying down, his face split in the widest grin imaginable. Her fingers were tapping her thighs as she rose up and down on her toes. What a thrill. Talk about being on a high.

Fergus looked as thrilled as she was. When he reached the platform and the two men grabbed him, he was laughing.

She threw herself at him, winding her arms around his shoulders. 'It was amazing.'

'Incredible.' He grabbed her, spun her in a circle before pulling her closer and leaned down. His mouth covered hers and his tongue dived inside—hot, delicious, thrilling.

Her head spun. Her mouth opened wider as she tasted him and drank in his heat, the whole wonder of Fergus. Fergus kissing her after all this time. Was this for real? Pressing her body harder against him to feel his body against hers, she kissed him back as though her life depended on it. Yes, very real. Awesomely so. Those muscles under her hands were firm and hot. His mouth tasted of wonder with an intensity she'd only known the first time they'd kissed.

Deep laughter around them interrupted her sense of wonder. Reluctantly she lifted her mouth to look around.

The two guys who had unhooked her from the harness were watching them with wide grins lighting up their dark faces. 'That's the best reaction to the ride we've seen in a while,' said one of them.

Fergus kept holding her. 'It was incredible,' he repeated.

She glanced at him. *Kissing me or the ride?* she wondered.

He winked. 'Both.'

Was she that obvious? Too bad. She couldn't always keep her feelings under lock and key when it came to Fergus. 'I agree.'

'I'll have to do the ride again. I missed everything on the way down, only felt the speed and wind and didn't notice much else.'

She had to *kiss* him again. But she agreed about the ride. 'There wasn't enough time to look around. Do you want to do it now? Or another time.'

'Another time. Something to look forward to.' He put his arm over her shoulders as he stood on one leg and freed the other from the harness tangled around his ankle. 'It's quite an adventure, isn't it?'

'Sure is.' She'd got a high from the zip line ride followed with a top-up from Fergus's kiss. Both experiences had been filled with excitement and amazement. 'What's next?'

'How about lunch at the first resort we come to?' He stepped away from the harness and straightened up, all but towering over her.

She usually disliked being small, as it made her think she had to prove she was big on the inside, but Fergus made her feel good about her size. She fitted against him perfectly. Taking a step back, she looked him over and felt her stomach tighten in anticipation. Of what, she wasn't sure, but that kiss surely wasn't a one-off. Not if she had anything to do with it. This man was coming up to her expectations of who she'd like in her life, at her side, permanently. She took another step backward. That was so wrong it was ridiculous. But why was it wrong? She hadn't been looking for a man to love and share her life with, yet Fergus got to her in so many unexpected ways she was confused—and happy. He already had her thinking he could help her get over the worry that she wasn't good enough to be in a relationship again. He'd turned his life around in the face of what must've been an overwhelming experience, yet he'd come out as an honest, genuine guy. Could he help her regain her confidence and turn her life around, too?

'Tamara? You're not keen?'

'What did you ask?'

'About lunch.'

They were always having meals together. Like an old couple with a regular routine. As if. 'I'm all for it. I'm starving after all the excitement.' Hungry for more than food, but she wouldn't mention that. Going too far, too soon, wasn't a good idea. There was a lot to think about first.

'For a moment there, I thought you must've left your brain halfway down the zip line.' The twinkle remained in his eyes, filling her with more longing for another kiss.

'Seriously, I'm in need of food in a relaxed setting with nothing more important to do than enjoy myself. And the company,' she added for the hell of it.

'When did you turn into such a charmer?' Fergus grinned.

'When bluntness doesn't work, it's always worth a try.'

'Your kiss worked.' He laughed. 'I can't imagine you do that often.'

She did a little wriggle on her toes. She was getting to like him more and more, and wanted that feeling to continue. More kisses included. 'I'll change out of my wet bikini before we go anywhere.' There was a changing room back at the start of the zip line.

His grin slipped. 'Okay.'

Her turn to laugh. 'Not saying I won't go swimming again, but I don't want my shirt sticking to my damp bikini top while I'm having lunch.' It would accentuate her boobs, and she'd probably struggle to eat, thinking about what lay beneath his shorts and T-shirt.

The wide smile returned. 'Come on, let's get moving. Want to walk back up or wait for the guys to give us a lift on the trailer?'

'Walk.' She'd try not to think what that smile might mean. Surely she wasn't getting to him in a sensual way? Then again, why not? He'd kissed her like he meant it and was hungry for more too.

The track back to the top was narrow, with loose pebbles making it slippery. When Fergus took her hand to steady her, she didn't pull away. Keeping her balance wasn't hard, but having his fingers entwined with hers sent shivers of desire down her spine. The zip line ride had excited her but the kiss that followed had really turned up the heat. Time to take a breath and slow down? There were still three weeks to get through, and if anything went wrong between them because they'd gone too far, it'd be difficult, if not impossible, to remain in accord while working alongside each other. And first and foremost, that was why they were here, not to begin a relationship.

But she wasn't letting his hand go. It felt right. So good. She'd never have thought holding hands could be such a turn-on. Hopefully, that was why

Fergus didn't let go until they reached the bike. Maybe he felt the same way.

Giving him a smile, she grabbed her bag to go change. 'Back in a minute.'

'No rush. We've got all day.'

That was the thing. They did. *I'm going to make the most of every hour with Fergus today.* If only to deepen their friendship. She laughed at herself. Who did she think she was fooling?

They spent the rest of the day at the first resort they came across. After helping her off the bike, Fergus kept his hands to himself, causing her to wonder if he'd been thinking along the same lines about how they had to stay on track if they wanted to get through their time here without any difficulties. Swallowing her disappointment, she stuck to her decision to make the most of being with him, enjoying the afternoon, swimming in the pool, sharing food platters and cold drinks. Like a real date. Being with Fergus was fun.

Even though her body was yearning for intimacy, her head worked hard to keep the desire in line. By the time Fergus parked outside their accommodation building at the end of the day, she was mentally exhausted but happier than she'd been in a long time.

'I'll take the bike back,' Fergus told her.

Stretching up on her tiptoes, she brushed a light kiss over his lips. 'Thanks for a wonderful day. See you in the morning.'

Placing his hands on either side of her head, he leaned in and deepened the kiss for a brief moment. '*Thank you.* I've had a lot of fun.' Turning around, he revved the motor and roared away.

Tamara watched him until the bike went around the corner. Her heart was beating hard, her face warm. 'So have I, Fergus. So have I.'

CHAPTER SEVEN

'THERE'S A TEAR HERE.' Fergus pressed hard on the vein leaking blood faster than a tap turned on full. He suspected there'd be more to come. A tree branch had rammed long-ways into the woman's abdomen when the ute she'd been driving went out of control on the coastal road and hit a tree.

'I'm getting more clamps,' Tamara told him, obviously thinking the same. She *should've* been a doctor.

'Good.' He continued investigating the damage in front of him.

Within moments Tamara was back. No messing around. Like the way she'd leapt up to kiss him on Sunday. No messing around then either. Heat ripped through him at the memory of her soft lips on his mouth. He couldn't deny she'd got to him. Was that good, or was it something to worry about?

'Here.' She slid the steel bowl onto the table.

'It's going to take lots of sutures to save the

uterus,' he said. 'Even then I'm not sure if she'll be able to conceive. The damage to the ovaries is extensive.'

Tamara shuddered. 'That's really sad.'

No identity had been made yet, but the woman looked to be in her late twenties or early thirties. 'I'd say she's had at least one baby.' The abdominal muscles were soft, suggesting a previous pregnancy.

'I hope she's already got the family she wants, then.'

'I agree.' The sadness emanating from Tamara again had him wondering if she wanted children. He could imagine her small figure swollen with a baby inside, and he smiled. It was a picture that filled him with a similar longing, but he shook it away. As if that was going to happen. He needed to get real. Tamara knew what had happened and still spent time with him, even kissed him, but did she still have doubts about how he'd turned out? About who he used to be? He couldn't be sure, and that was the problem. But he wasn't getting a lot of say in how he felt about Tamara. She was taking over his mind all too easily. As well as other parts of his body, if he was being honest.

Suturing the internal wounds took time and care, and gave him something else to concentrate on rather than the gorgeous nurse on the other side of the table. When he finally straightened from the table, his patient was in better shape than when she'd been brought in by the paramedics. 'She's going to need blood,' he said.

Ian looked up from the monitors. 'We don't have a big blood bank, so I hope she's got a common group.'

'Surely O positive will be available?'

'Should be, but you'll have to get onto it sooner rather than later,' Ian warned.

'I'm O pos,' Tamara piped up. 'Happy to donate if needed.'

'I'll keep that in mind when I see the lab techs. Which'll be shortly. I want to make sure everything's all right here first.' He couldn't be too careful when it came to trauma cases. He hadn't known what to expect when he'd opened the already torn abdominal area, but he needed to be absolutely certain he'd done all he could. 'How's the blood pressure?'

'Eighty-six over fifty-eight,' Ian said.

'Could be worse considering the blood loss.' Fergus began to relax. Tossing his gloves in the bin, he said, 'You can start bringing her round. I'll go arrange the blood transfusion. Tamara, are you sure you don't mind donating, if needed?'

'Wouldn't have said it if I didn't mean it,' she retorted.

'True.'

Her eyebrows rose, then she appeared to smile behind her mask. 'Go get things sorted.'

'I'd like you to stay with this lady until I get

back. Don't take her to recovery. She's bound to be in shock when she comes round and as she won't know where she is since she was unconscious when they brought her in, having you here to answer questions would be a help.' She could do that in recovery, but it was busy out there.

'No problem.' Tamara was watching the woman as Ian began reversing the anaesthetic.

As easy as that. If only everything was so straightforward when it came to Tamara. Like getting closer without worrying about the past coming back to bite his arse. Because everything kept coming back to his father, he often felt worthless as an individual despite holding his head high and fighting the consequences. But after Harriet's betrayal, he doubted if he could ever truly trust someone to love him for himself. If he did manage to put it all behind him.

Many people had deserted him when he'd needed them most. To find the love he yearned for, he had to take another chance on being loved unconditionally. Was he capable of doing that? He just didn't know.

Tamara hoped no one noticed her yawning behind her mask. With the woman involved in the accident needing urgent surgery first thing, it had become another long day as they worked through the schedule. She hadn't had to donate blood as there was enough available in the lab.

Fergus had refused to cancel any operations even after he'd learned they had an emergency to deal with as well. She'd been right behind him. They were here to do all they could for the locals. If that meant being exhausted at the end of each day, then she'd cope. There hadn't been a lot of sleep going on all week. Daydreaming about Fergus and what it would be like to have more of those kisses and to be held against his naked body had taken over from the humidity. Whatever was going on in her head and heart, she had it bad.

One more procedure to do before their day was done. Belle, their final patient of the day, was dozing while she waited to be taken into Theatre.

'Belle, it's time.' Tamara shook her arm gently.

Her eyes blinked open. 'Wish you were waking me to say the surgery was finished,' she said.

So do I, thought Tamara. 'You've been very patient,' she said.

'It's okay. I'm not an urgent case like Aria was.'

'You've heard about the woman in the accident this morning?'

'Her kids go to the same school as ours. Is she going to be all right?'

'She's had surgery and is resting quietly.'

'In other words, that's all you're going to say.' Belle nodded. 'I understand.'

'Let's get you into Theatre so the anaesthetist can have a quick chat with you.' Tamara released the brake and began rolling the bed through the doors. 'Doctor Collier's waiting for you too.'

'I am popular.'

Tamara laughed. She liked this woman. 'You've got their full attention. Make the most of it.'

'What's funny, ladies?' Fergus asked as she lined up the bed beside the table.

'Girl talk,' Belle told him.

'You're supposed to be half asleep by now.' Fergus chuckled.

'Belle, I'm Ian, your anaesthetist during the operation. Do you have any concerns about having anaesthetic?'

Thankfully, they were back on track or it'd be midnight before they were finished up. Tamara sighed. Tomorrow, five more ops were scheduled. Then it would be Sunday again.

So far, she had no plans for the day off. Lazing round on the beach was tempting. Also a second zip line ride. But she might save that for the last weekend here. Something to look forward to. Unless Fergus suggested they do it again tomorrow, and then she'd be buzzing. For another crazy ride and another knee-bending kiss or two.

Once Belle was lying on the operating table Tamara covered her with a sheet and squeezed her hand. 'See you soon.'

'Not too soon, I hope.'

'Start counting to ten, Belle,' Ian said.

'One, two, three, four—'

'Gone,' Tamara said as she tapped the back of Belle's hand to be certain. Placing the blood pressure cuff around Belle's arm, she pumped it tight and read the monitor. 'Normal.'

'Ready,' Ian said.

Fergus picked up a scalpel. 'Me too.'

Swabs in hand, Tamara waited as Fergus opened Belle's abdomen. 'You've done a few of these hysterectomies over the past couple of weeks.' The days were flying past. She couldn't believe they were already halfway through their time. The thought of returning home and not seeing Fergus was an increasing worry. He was coming to mean so much to her. Too much. She needed to be incredibly careful or she could get badly hurt again.

'*We* have,' he corrected her.

She liked that he didn't take all the credit, even when he did most of the work. She was the cleaner-upper and loved it. It was nursing at an intensity that kept her focused. When she was doing her nursing training, she'd thought she'd work on wards looking after people when they were recovering from an illness or surgery, but Theatre had drawn her in from the outset. She cared for patients at a time when they were worried about being put under anaesthetic and having surgery. Over here, she often saw them afterwards too, which she liked.

'Swabs, Tamara.' Fergus stood back for a moment to watch her clean around the opening he'd made.

When he removed the uterus, she held out a steel bowl for him to place it in, then put it aside to swab before handing him a suture threaded needle. It was a routine she knew well and found almost relaxing. Of course, she was aware things could go wrong fast, but she was ready to do whatever required if that happened.

Together they worked on Belle's abdomen until Fergus had closed the wound and she'd finished swabbing the area clean. Standing back, they both watched Ian reverse the anaesthesia. Then Tamara wheeled Belle out to recovery to wait until she was awake and feeling all right.

The day was finally over.

'You still think you'll do more volunteering after this?' Fergus asked as they drank coffee, overlooking the hospital grounds while waiting for Tim and Sarah.

'Definitely. I get a buzz from helping others less fortunate. As soon I get home, I'm putting my name down for next year. You're right. What we're doing is wonderful in a different way to how I usually feel about nursing. I feel more involved with these people.' Everyone was so welcoming and grateful, it was humbling.

'You found your calling, didn't you?'

'I certainly did. I'd say the same about you after seeing how you look out for your patients, whether they're awake or under anaesthetic.' He was always careful and gentle when operating. As were most surgeons she'd worked with, but Fergus seemed even more concerned when it came to surgeries. Maybe she was looking for all things good about him.

'I do my best.'

An understatement if ever she'd heard one. 'Was it always your intention to become a doctor when you were at college?'

'Yes, it was. Though back then, I thought I'd become a heart surgeon.' His smile was lopsided. 'Then one day in my first year at university, one of the women studying with me said her father was a cardiologist and that it was one of the most admired positions. That's when I took a long, hard look at what I really wanted from my career, and after listening to a friend talk about the problems she and her partner were facing trying to get pregnant, I knew I wanted to be a gynaecologist.'

The way he was opening up more and more suggested he trusted her not to give him a hard time about the past. 'You got it right. The patients you've worked with here all say you're wonderful.' There hadn't been one who'd complained about what he'd done for them. 'A lot of that's how you take the time to talk the procedures through and listen to any questions or concerns they have without looking at your watch.' She'd seen specialists do that in pre-Theatre rooms and it drove her crazy. Patients were vulnerable pre-op and deserved to be heard, even if the clock was ticking in Theatre.

Fergus smiled. 'You're saying not all surgeons are the same?'

'Sometimes, I think trainee doctors need to do a paper on how to be nice to patients, but I'm being unfair because most I've worked with are definitely kind and caring.'

'Like nurses.'

'You're on to it.'

'So why is nursing your dream job like you said at the airport?'

Tamara didn't have to think about it. 'I was always going to be a nurse. I've never regretted my choice. I wonder if I got Dad's compassionate gene. He raised Sashi and me so lovingly that we couldn't have asked for better. Other than to have our mother back,' she added quietly. Then shook her head. Where did that come from? She never said out loud how much she'd missed her mum growing up.

A warm hand covered hers. 'You've had your share of tragedy.'

'I have, but like I said, Dad was awesome.'

'You miss him a lot.'

Oh, damn and blast. Something else she didn't like to talk about. It was too soon and still raw.

Fergus squeezed her hand. 'It's all right. You don't have to say anything.'

It might be good to talk about it, let go of some of the pain. 'Dad suffered from stage-four bowel cancer. When he was told there was nothing more to be done for him, I took a leave of absence from work and nursed him at home, because he didn't want to be anywhere else but where he lived with my mum, and where Sashi and I grew up.'

Her hand was back in Fergus's. 'That's special.'

'It was.'

'I can't begin to imagine how you coped.'

He'd lost his father in totally different circumstances, and she didn't know anything about his relationship with his mother. They might've become closer while dealing with the situation. 'Does anyone know what they'll do in that situation?' she asked.

'No.' Blunt. And poignant. He sounded like he hadn't got over what he'd lost. Not completely anyway. Probably never would.

Her turn to squeeze Fergus's hand. She had no other answer without getting too deep, and that was something she wasn't ready for. Losing her father had been huge. After how John had treated her, the loss of Dad had only underlined what could happen if she gave her heart to anyone again. Sashi had said she was wrong to believe she should hold back on that score because love was everyone's dream, and essential for a fulfilling life. Seeing how happy her sister was with her man and their kids, Tamara knew she was right, but it didn't help to lift her caution. Losing a loved one hurt like hell.

'You all right?' he asked.

'Actually, I am.' She meant it. Whatever lay ahead, she'd relish this time with Fergus. 'I don't usually talk about Dad, but I'm glad I did.'

'I'm here any time you want to get anything off your chest.'

She liked that. In fact, she was liking everything about him. Scary and exhilarating all in one. Life could be looking up.

'You've got it bad,' Tim said when they climbed out of the van laden with takeout meals Sarah and Tamara had left them to take inside.

'You think?' Fergus shrugged, pretending a nonchalance he didn't feel. Despite warning himself more than once, Tamara dominated his thinking whenever he wasn't focused on work. Even then she managed to sneak into his head at times.

'Definitely. You're not very good at hiding your feelings.'

'Here I thought I was very accomplished at doing that.' What if Tamara was the one for him? She'd known him when everything had turned on its head and had never given him a hard time about his father. *No, 'the one' doesn't exist, remember?*

Tim laughed, shaking his head. 'Often, yes, but when it comes to Tamara, you're up the creek without a paddle.'

Wonderful. 'I hope she hasn't noticed whatever it is you think you have.' He doubted she had. She was too busy keeping her own feelings under control. There were moments when he knew she wanted to get close, to touch him, maybe repeat that kiss, but she always pulled her shoulders back and put on a straight face whenever he thought she might be letting go a little. Which wound him up harder than her dazzling eyes did. He *couldn't* risk falling for her. Not when love wasn't supposed to be on his agenda at all.

In the kitchen, Tamara handed him a plate. 'What are you doing for Christmas?'

Christmas was only weeks away. 'I haven't given it a lot of thought.'

'What do you usually do?' she asked.

'Spend it with my grandparents. Though now they live in a retirement home in Nelson, my grandma has given up making her hot ham and roast vegetables.' He smacked his lips together. 'Always my favourite.'

'Because your grandmother cooked it, I bet. I prefer turkey. It's the only time of the year I have it, and even then not every year. Depends on my sister and what she has planned.'

'Do you go to her place for the day?'

'Always.' Tamara's face dropped. 'It'll be different this year with Dad gone.'

He'd love to hug her, but after Tim's comment he stayed where he was. 'Your sister lives in Nelson, right?' Maybe they could catch up when he went down to see his grandparents.

'Yes, thank goodness. It's always a great time with the kids excited about Santa and presents.' That longing in her voice when she mentioned her sister's children had returned.

He wanted to tell her she'd surely be a mum one day, but he wouldn't. What if the longing was brought on by the fact she couldn't have children? When it came down to it, he knew so little about her. Only one way to find out, though, and that meant spending more time together. 'I'll be in Nelson for a couple of days, so let's catch up,' he offered impulsively, which wasn't at all like him.

'You're on.'

An unexpected sense of relief filled him. He hadn't believed she'd say a flat-out no, but to hear her agreement felt surprisingly good. 'Great.' Looking across the room, he got a wink from Tim. *Thanks, buddy*, he muttered under his breath. Hopefully Tamara hadn't seen it. 'What have you two got planned?'

'Making the most of not working,' Tim said.

'A family get-together,' Sarah added. 'I've got three brothers who are married with kids so it's always a noisy, cheerful day.'

A yearning for children to celebrate all the wonderful events that happened throughout the year was rising again. Tamara was stirring up so many feelings he'd buried when he and Harriet broke up. But the idea of possibly having a partner and children made him remember what he'd risked all those years ago, which had nearly broken him when Harriet had walked away. A shiver went down his spine.

CHAPTER EIGHT

TAMARA JERKED UPRIGHT in her bed. 'What the hell?' It sounded like a freight train was rolling down the road below her window.

A familiar sound. She knew exactly what it was. An earthquake. A huge one. She leapt off the bed. The building started shaking violently. The walls creaked. The ceiling groaned as though about to implode. Staying upright on the heaving floor was a struggle. The noise grew louder as plates and mugs crashed to the floor. She needed to get in the doorway. Or down on her knees with her head under her arms. This was bad.

Crash. The bathroom door fell inwards.

She shrieked. 'Fergus.'

'I'm here, Tamara,' Fergus called from the other side of the wall. 'I'm coming.'

The floor moved up and down and sideways. 'Stop,' she shouted. Every second felt like a minute. Books fell off the table, then banged onto the floor. Her sandals slid across the room, then came back towards her.

'Fergus,' she screamed again. She was terrified. She wanted it to end. Now. Slip-sliding across the rocking room, she tried to open the door. No go. Jammed shut. 'I can't get out.' Panic filled her. She couldn't stay here. She was tugging with all her might, but it stayed put.

Suddenly the shaking stopped. All went quiet. Too quiet. The quake was over. Until the aftershocks started. Then they'd go through the same scenario many times more. With less intensity, if they were lucky. She'd been through the Christchurch earthquake years back and knew what lay ahead. Hell. The worst thing being there was nothing anyone could do to stop the quakes.

'Fergus, I need you,' she whispered. 'I don't want to be alone.'

'Tamara, are you all right?' Fergus banged her door with his fist. It didn't budge.

'No, I'm not. I hate these things.' The fear in her voice made his heart trip.

Tamara was tough, but this was something totally out of her hands. She wouldn't like that. Nor the consequences that could follow. He wasn't exactly enjoying himself either, but his biggest concern was Tamara. Her fear was gut-wrenching. He had to get her out so they could make their way downstairs and outside. 'Stand back. I'm going to kick your door in.' It could work or go badly for him.

'It's jammed,' she shouted.

'Are you out of the way?'

'Yes.' Were those tears in her voice?

He hoped not. They'd be hard to take. 'Here I come,' he called. She might've said she was out of the way, but he was making sure. Slamming the door into her was not an option. Standing back, he lifted his leg and went for it.

The door groaned and moved slightly.

'And again,' he called.

This time the door fell in, with him sprawled on top.

Tamara was instantly reaching for him. 'Fergus? Are you all right?'

'Yes. What about you? You weren't injured?'

'Apart from being terrified, I'm good. I loathe earthquakes. I was in Christchurch when they had the big one and this felt worse. The noise of it coming woke me and I immediately knew what was happening.'

'I've never been in one that big. We need a torch.'

'I haven't got one. Have you?'

'On my bedside table.'

'I'll get it.'

'No, Tamara, I don't want you going anywhere on your own. We stick together. I doubt we can trust any part of the building not to give way. Give me a hand up.'

She reached out her hands to take his. She was

shaking hard. 'Come on. As much as I want to go get that torch, I don't want to move far from you.'

He wrapped her in a hug. For both of them. 'We got through it. We'll get through anything else that follows.'

Her head lay on his bare chest, her hot breath sharp stabs on his skin. 'I hate earthquakes,' she repeated.

'Probably because we can't do a damned thing about them.'

Her head moved up and down against him. 'Yes.'

'Hey, Fergus, Tamara. You guys all right?' Tim called from the other side of the hallway, a torch beam finding them.

'Think so. What about you two?'

'Sarah took a knock on the head when the mirror came off the wall. From what I can see, she's not seriously injured. We need to get out of here.'

'I'm going to find my torch and take a look around.' What if they couldn't get out of the building? They'd find a way. They had to. There'd be aftershocks coming.

'Tell me where it is and I'll get it. Sarah, come out here with the others. We have to stick together.'

'It was on the bedside table. Could be anywhere now.'

Sarah quickly joined them. 'The sooner we're

out of this building the better as far as I'm concerned. It's not very stable.'

'I agree. I imagine our services are going to be needed at the hospital after this. I'm heading that way once we've got out.'

'As if you wouldn't,' Tamara muttered.

Despite everything he grinned. 'I like that you believe in me.'

Tim returned. 'Here you go. One torch. Now what? Do we get our phones and other gear or try to make our way out of the building and hope we can get everything later?'

'I'm all for getting out,' Tamara was quick to answer.

The building creaked and groaned, and Fergus had to agree with her. 'Better to be safe than sorry.' He took a look at her, and then across at Tim and Sarah. 'Think we need to grab some clothes. None of us are dressed to go out on the street.' Fergus shook his head. Tamara looked so damned sexy in a pink singlet and white satin knickers, it was hard to focus on the mess they were in. Then he realised he wore only a pair of lightweight shorts that barely covered his butt.

Tim nodded. 'Good point. Let's do that. Might as well grab essentials while we're at it.'

'I'll come with you, Tamara.' She wasn't going into her room on her own. 'Don't argue. That'd only waste time.'

'I wasn't going to.'

Within minutes everyone had returned to the hall dressed in hurriedly hauled-on clothes and carrying tote bags. They moved to the stairway, Fergus with Tamara's hand in his, just as Tim had Sarah's.

The stairs looked all right, but caution prevailed. 'One of us should go down first to make certain they're safe.'

'I'll go,' Tamara said. 'I'm the lightest.'

She was right about that, but he didn't want her going first.

'Let's do this.' She removed her hand from his grasp.

'I'm right behind you,' Sarah said.

Someone shouted from below, 'Hey, Docs, you guys there?'

'We're making our way down now.'

'Go easy. Lots of damage to this building.'

'Great,' Fergus muttered.

The stairs creaked with every step they took. Eventually they reached the ground floor and hurried out onto the street to be greeted by a fireman.

'Glad you're all okay,' the man said. 'We've barely started checking on people, but some are already making their way to hospital with injuries. Many buildings came down.'

The ground started shaking again.

Fergus caught Tamara to him and held her tight. 'It's okay, Tamara. We're out of the building.'

'We're not supposed to stand out on a street lined with tall buildings. It's dangerous.'

The shaking stopped and he leaned back to look into her eyes. 'You're doing well. Want to go to the hospital and see how we can help?'

She straightened immediately. 'Of course.' Nurse to the fore. Hopefully caring for others would help keep her focused and her mind away from the earthquake.

'Tim, Sarah, what do you think?' he asked.

'Same as you. We need to make ourselves available.'

The fireman stepped up. 'I'll give you a ride. We'll have to take the long way round.'

'Is there a lot of damage?' Tim asked.

He nodded slowly. 'From the calls already coming through the radios I'd say so. Our buildings aren't all as solidly built as they should be. Not enough money to go round.'

'It can't be helped,' Fergus told him. Sometimes they got it wrong back home too. Especially when it came to the older buildings.

The man shrugged. 'Come on, let's get you somewhere safer.'

They climbed into the fire department jeep and stared out the windows as they headed to the hospital. Collapsed buildings, huge cracks in the roads and people wandering around in a daze were all over the place.

Beside him, Tamara was shivering. He tucked

her in against his side. 'Deep breaths. We'll get through this.'

'I know, but what about the families who live along the roads? All those cute little kids must be terrified.'

So she was thinking about them and not her own reactions. That would help keep her calm. 'It's unavoidable.'

'I remember after the Christchurch earthquake how people were too scared to go inside their homes for days, while others carried on as normal, allowing for the lack of water and other essentials as they went.'

'And you?'

'Did my best to carry on regardless. For four days I worked all hours in the medical tents set up in Hagley Park.' She gave him a tentative smile. 'I know how this goes, but I did lose it for a bit back there in the apartment.'

'Shows you're normal.' He smiled, hoping to lift her spirits. If only he could swing her up in his arms and take her away from this.

'You weren't with us,' Tim said. 'Sarah's tougher than me. Despite the mirror whacking her, she insisted on checking me over when the shaking stopped.'

Finally, after a convoluted trip on destroyed roads, they reached the hospital, where crowds were gathering outside the main entrance. People lay on the ground, while others walked back and forth between everyone. Lights showed through the windows. Torches were being waved around. The clear sky made the darkness less intense. One plus in everyone's favour.

'Here you go, folks. For everyone's sake, I hope you don't have too many injured people to deal with.' The fireman pulled up as close to the door as he could get.

Fergus got out and looked around. 'They've obviously got a generator to make life easier.'

'Three, actually.'

'Well prepared then,' Tim commented.

'This isn't the first quake to strike Vanuatu, and no doubt won't be the last, but in my experience it's the worst.'

'Thanks for the ride.' Tamara got out and looked around at the crowd watching them.

'I'll see you all later. I'll find out more about the building you were using and let you know if it's safe to get all your belongings out. It might pay to see if you can sleep here for a night or two.' The fireman drove off slowly, stopping to talk to people as he went.

'Shouldn't he be rushing to see what needs to be done urgently?' Sarah asked.

'Talking to people might help calm them, and that's just as important as anything else,' Tim replied.

'Let's see what's going on inside.' Fergus took Tamara's hand again and walked towards the main door. There was nothing to be gained by standing out here. He was ready to get busy dealing with injuries because he didn't believe for one minute there wouldn't be plenty. The decimated buildings, some flattened, that they'd passed on the way had turned his mouth acidic. It was horrific. There was no way people had got out unhurt from some of those buildings. No doubt there'd be deaths.

'Slow down, Fergus,' Tim called.

'You tell him.' Tamara was holding his hand as though she never intended letting go. 'At least I'm experienced in the aftermath of an earthquake.'

Tamara shook her head. How she'd have got through the last hour without Fergus at her side, she'd never know. He'd been there for her from the moment she'd called out to him. Now she needed to toughen up and get on with being a nurse, not a woman relying on a man to get her through the coming hours. Reluctantly letting go of his hand, she followed him inside, ready to do whatever was required to help others. It was the only way to get over the quake. Focusing on other people and their injuries would shove her fright to the back of her mind, and with a bit of luck that's where it'd stay. 'Going to ED first?'

'Where else?' Fergus asked.

'You know me. I like to be sure.' She was walking close to him because she needed his strength, liked how he'd held her in the jeep and the other moments he'd touched her. He'd made her feel safe. She didn't feel ashamed for being afraid. She could pick up spiders, catch rats in a trap, go to the top of high buildings, but earthquakes were her uncomfortable place.

'In here.' He pushed open a door.

Raised voices slammed into them like a wall of noise. Doctors and nurses were rushing between beds and chairs where patients waited anxiously. Some lay on the floor as there was nowhere else to go.

'How did they get here so soon?' she wondered.

'They'll be locals from nearby. Plus, it's now an hour since the quake struck.'

She looked around for someone in charge. 'That man standing by the desk seems to be running the show.'

'I agree.' Fergus turned back to Sarah and Tim. 'What do you think?'

Tim nodded. 'Afu's the head man in ED.'

Afu spotted them. Relief lightened his taut face.

'Afu, we're here to help in any capacity you need us,' Tim said. 'This is Sarah, my wife. She's a nurse, as is Tamara. Fergus is a gynaecologist who can help in any way you require, though not major surgeries, other than for women with problems in the reproductive area, which I'm presuming won't be many.'

'Hopefully not, but we've got plenty to keep you busy, Fergus.' Afu shook hands with them all. 'There're fractures, minor head wounds and other injuries. There're also two people with internal problems yet to be sorted.'

'Currently our ED doctors are in different cubicles with a nurse each. I'd suggest you all take a cubicle. For safety reasons, emergency crews are setting up tents outside with beds and equipment, but until they're ready we're working inside. There's no other choice if we're to saves lives.'

'Makes perfect sense,' Fergus said. 'Tamara, you okay working with me?'

Try to keep her away. 'Absolutely.'

Despite the tense atmosphere, Sarah smiled. 'Who else is she going to work with? I'm going to stick with Tim as much as possible.'

Tamara hoped being with Fergus would make that safe feeling last the distance. She walked into the nearest cubicle with no medical staff attending the wee boy lying on the bed in his mother's arms. 'Hello, I'm Tamara. I'm a nurse. What's your name, little man?'

The boy blinked, then turned his head into his mother's breast.

'He's call Fuifui,' the woman told her. 'He fell

out of the top bunk in the earthquake. His brother said he landed on his shoulder and head.'

Tamara crouched down beside the bed. 'Fuifui, does your head hurt?'

He nodded slowly without looking at her.

'Thank you for telling me. This is Doctor Fergus. He's going to check you over. Do you know what a doctor is?'

A more vigorous nod. His head couldn't be hurting too badly if he could nod like that.

Fergus stood by the bed. 'Hello, Fuifui. Does your shoulder hurt?'

'Yes.'

'It's a strange shape,' the mother said.

'Can you lie beside your mum so I can look at it, Fuifui?'

Tamara helped the boy move onto the mattress, his face screwed tight and tears leaking down his cheeks.

Tamara wiped his face gently. 'Bruising above his right eye,' she told Fergus.

'Same side as the shoulder.' He felt over and around the shoulder. 'Dislocated. I'll give him a local anaesthetic before I do something about that, but first I need to check his skull for soft spots.' Again those long fingers went to work, touching every part of Fuifui's head.

The boy yelped when Fergus touched behind his right ear.

'Sorry, mate. You're going to have a bit of a

headache for a few days, otherwise I think your head's all right.' He looked to the mother. 'He's got bruises around his ear. The bigger problem is his shoulder. It's dislocated,' he repeated. 'Do you understand what that means?'

'Yes. Can you force it back in place or does he need surgery?'

'Since it's only just happened, I should be able to put it back into place without surgery. It's a painful process so I need your permission to give him a mild drug to make him sleep, followed by a light anaesthesia so he doesn't feel a thing.'

'Go ahead. Do I have to sign anything?'

'I presume so. It's normal to do that back where we come from. I imagine it's the same here. I'll go and arrange everything.'

Tamara began wiping Fuifui's face clean. He looked like he'd been swimming in a mud pool, not sleeping in bed. 'Kids, eh?'

'He's not good at doing what he's told.' His mum smiled lovingly at her son.

'He's a boy. That's how they're made.' And lots of girls she'd dealt with in emergency departments. 'Have you any daughters, too?' *Keep talking and forget the quakes.* As if.

'Two girls, two boys.' Her smile widened.

'All set to go.' Fergus strode into the cubicle with a dish containing pills and a vial of anaesthesia.

'Mum, we need you to sit on the chair while we do this.'

As soon as Fuifui nodded off, Fergus manipulated the shoulder back in place and bound it firmly against his body with a crepe bandage. 'There you go, little man. No jumping off anything high for a few days.'

'You need to tell him when he's awake.' His mother chuckled. 'He won't listen to me.'

'He might. It'll be very tender,' Fergus told her. 'We'll be back to check on Fuifui before you take him home.'

'Thank you very much for looking after my boy.'

'No problem.' His heart went out to these stoic people. 'Take care out there.'

'Let's find another cubicle and see who's next,' Fergus said to Tamara. She looked so much better now that she had other things to focus on. Her gorgeous smile was back and the tension in her shoulders had disappeared. 'It's going to be a long night.'

Fergus got that right, Tamara thought as she dropped blood-soaked swabs into a bin. She'd lost count of how many patients they'd seen. The last woman had come in bleeding after a window broke over her during a big aftershock. The shards had caused deep cuts on her face, neck, shoulders, arms. It had taken Fergus time to suture them but now he was done. 'I wonder what's next?' she said out loud.

'Coffee and something to eat,' he answered as he looked out the window. 'The sun's been up for ages. We need a break.'

'That's the best thing I've heard for hours.'

They found Tim and Sarah at a table in the canteen and joined them with sandwiches and mugs of tea. 'How's it going in Theatre?' Tamara asked.

'Busy, but it finally seems to be slowing down,' Tim said. 'Did you hear the quake was a magnitude seven point three?'

Tamara's mouth dried. 'That's humungous.' Her body tensed as she remembered the shaking as the floor rose and fell beneath her. There'd been numerous quakes since then, and she doubted they'd stop any time soon.

'It explains the strong aftershocks,' Fergus said.

He'd touched her every time one struck, helping her find her inner strength again. 'I wonder if that fireman has found us somewhere to stay.' Somewhere that didn't shake would be perfect. And impossible.

'I'm not going back to the apartments.' Sarah was adamant.

She shivered. 'Me either. But what options have we got if he doesn't come up with somewhere? He'll be too busy doing essential work.

We can't stay here. All the beds and floor space are taken.'

Carrie, the nurse Tamara had met on the first day, was walking past. She stopped and came back. 'I overheard what you said. Jimmy, my husband, is the fireman who gave you a lift earlier. He's checking out places for you as he goes around the town. It'll most likely be a resort or hotel as no new visitors will be arriving for a while.'

'That would be great.' People around here were kind even in the middle of a disaster.

Carrie nodded. 'I'll go and call Jimmy on the radio to tell him you're happy with the plan.'

'The only problem there,' Tamara said, 'Is if tourists can't fly in, then the ones already here can't get out. There might not be any rooms available.'

More hours and many more patients later, Fergus went to find Tamara who had been assisting Tim and Sarah with a surgery on a middle-aged man who'd fallen off a roof onto a garden post while trying to fix broken roof tiles. She looked as shattered as he felt. Placing an arm around her waist he pulled her into a hug. 'What's up?'

'The man died. He bled out, despite everything Tim did.'

'Come on, everyone. Afu says to get away for a break while we can. We've got accommodation at a nearby resort and it's time to get out of here. We've done more than enough for now.'

Tamara sagged against him. 'Yes, please.'

'You're asleep on your feet, my friend,' he said, though it felt like she was something more than a friend now. He didn't want to go back to where he'd been before they'd caught up. It was rather lonely there.

'You don't look a lot better.'

'Let's get out of here before someone else asks for help.' He cared that Tamara was coping with everything while looking shattered beyond recognition. In the emergency department she'd been calm and confident, but whenever she stopped to take a breath, he saw her looking around as though wondering what was coming next. Not once had he ever seen her so concerned about anything. He was going to stick by her until she found her feet again. Of course, if asked, she'd deny she'd lost them, so he'd remain quiet on that subject. They were doing better by the day, and he'd do nothing to wreck that.

He was so aware of Tamara that nothing else got to him, not even the continuing quakes or the endless stream of patients. She was sexy and he desired her. She cared not only for patients, but about them. She was sharp and intelligent, liked keeping fit and having fun. She also liked challenges. In other words, Tamara was his kind of woman. A wake-up call he hadn't seen coming.

After Harriet, he'd dated quite a few women, but not one of them had him thinking beyond a fling. He wasn't even having a fling with Tamara, yet here he was wondering what it would be like to spend more time with her doing the things they both enjoyed.

They stepped outside and were immediately swamped with humidity. 'Just what we need,' he muttered.

A four-wheel-drive truck pulled up, Jimmy behind the wheel. 'Hop in, guys. I'll drop you off at your accommodation. It's at a resort nearby.'

'You're a champ, mate. By the way, I'm Fergus and this is Tamara, and Sarah and Tim. We didn't get around to introducing ourselves last time.'

'Don't worry, we had more important things to think about. I'm taking a break once I've dropped you off. It's hell out there, but I think we've dealt with the most urgent problems for now.'

'What about tourists? I presume the airport's closed,' Tamara said.

'It is and will be for a few days for commercial flights, but it's open for humanitarian flights. The Australian Air Force is sending planes over with essential relief cargo and people to give a hand with roads and the runway, et cetera. New Zealand's arranging similar aid.' He carried on talking about what he'd seen and done over the preceding hours until they reached the resort.

'Here you go, folks. Try to have a comfortable night.'

At the reception desk the manager greeted them like long-lost friends. 'Welcome to the Beach House. I'm Harry. Thank you for what you've been doing for our people. It's much appreciated.' He placed key cards on the desk. 'We've got two units ready for you, and the kitchen's open and will provide dinner or any other food you need. Can't guarantee what you'll get, but it will be well cooked.'

Two rooms. Single or double beds? Fergus glanced at Tamara and saw the same question on her face. Which did she want? Or did she want a room of her own? 'Tamara?'

Her steady gaze locked on him. 'I'm fine with that.'

He knew she wasn't talking about the kitchen being open. Heat fizzed along his veins, knocking the exhaustion aside. It had been one hell of a twenty-odd hours with the quakes constantly reminding them what they had no control over as they faced a myriad of patients requiring all their attention. He had to let go and relax or he'd not be able to crawl out of bed in the morning for another round of injured people. And Tamara held the answer to that in her hand.

If she was on the same page as him.

'By the way,' Harry called. 'Jimmy retrieved your gear from your apartments and brought it here.' He indicated a stack of bags. 'No idea whose is whose.'

'The man's a wonder,' Tamara commented as she swung her pack over her shoulder. 'Glad I've got something to wear that doesn't smell of sweat.'

If he had his way, whatever she got into, it wouldn't stay on for long.

Tamara watched Fergus tap the key card against the lock, her heart pounding. She was about to share a room with the one man she'd never believed she'd get this close to. The man she'd once had the hots for and a longing to get up close and personal with, and she had done everything possible to hide from those feelings.

Not anymore. Not since arriving here, really. Time to get real about her feelings. Lying to hide them from herself was a waste of time and energy and had only created more problems than the truth. So honestly? She wanted him. Of course, she was tired beyond description, but that wasn't why she felt this way. Fergus had been there for her from the moment the apartment building began shaking and he hadn't gone far from her side since. Whenever fear had hit her, he'd been there, holding her or talking her through the moment. Whether he'd also been afraid, she didn't know. He hadn't shown fear, nor had he been tense when he held her.

'Tamara? It's not too late to see if there's another room for one of us.' Fergus was watching her with a longing she hadn't seen before. Not even back when they were teens pretending they didn't really care about each other.

Grabbing his hand, she tugged him into the room and kicked the door closed behind them. 'It's way too late for that.' Stretching up on her tiptoes, she found his mouth and kissed him. Long, and hot, and with everything she had to give. Oh, it felt so damned wonderful. He tasted exotic. Turned every part of her on fire with the need to forget the horrors of the past night and day. Had her aching to have him inside her, to finally know him intimately. To lose herself in Fergus would be bliss. And a lot more, no doubt.

He was returning her kiss as fervently. Which thrilled her to bits. There was no stopping either of them. He clearly needed this as much as she did. Perfect. She'd waited so long for this. Lifting one leg, she stretched it to curl it around his waist.

Fergus lifted her higher, making it easier to wrap both legs around him. His hands spread firmly over her backside as she nestled closer to his wide, firm chest and all the time he kissed her deeper, almost devouring her in his bid to get more of her. And winding her tighter than she'd believed possible. This was unbelievable. She'd never known sex could be this amazing, and they hadn't even got started yet. It was mind-blowing. Every cell in her body was crying out for more.

Any moment now she was going to explode with need if they didn't move to the bed. Lifting her head, she locked her eyes on his hot gaze. 'Fergus? I can't wait much longer.'

A slow, crooked smile widened his mouth and sent another wave of heat fizzing through her. 'Know what you mean,' he whispered hoarsely. 'But we're going to slow down and make the most of every touch, every moment.'

'I—I can't,' she croaked through the need filling her.

Fergus strode across the room and lowered her onto the bed before dropping his shorts and hauling his shirt over his head. Lying beside her, he held her close, his hands pushing under her clothes for his fingers to run over her skin, heating her up further, yet quietening her racing hormones so she assimilated more of him. Her own hands were working on his skin, touching him everywhere, feeling his muscles, his strength, then his erection. He was ready for her. She melted into him, savouring each touch, each moment, everything about Fergus.

Sprawling over him, his hardness pressing against her drove her to new heights of desire. 'Fergus, I want you,' she murmured.

His hands were making light work of removing her shirt, touching her breasts as he went. Shivers of pleasure rippled through her as his fingers stroked down over her stomach. Then lower and lower, sliding beneath her shorts.

Reaching for his length, she rubbed gently, slowly, causing him to strain against her.

'Tamara,' he groaned, then flipped her onto the bed and rose above her to remove the last of her clothing.

Her gaze fixed on his need for her. And deep inside something gave way, letting Fergus in more than ever. Letting her accept she could make this work, make him happy, because he wanted her as much as she wanted him.

Lifting her legs she wrapped them around him to keep him close, to feel his heat against her core.

He settled between her legs, his hands again working magic on her breasts, then her stomach and lower. Then finally when she couldn't take any more, he touched her where she was most sensitive. She cried out, 'Fergus. Please. Fergus!'

Lifting her hips she reached out to pull him closer to her heat.

As he slid inside her, she cried out again, 'Fergus! Yes.'

She climaxed instantly. Then he was with her, moving into her heat, pulling back, pushing in again. In, out, in, out, reaching his own pinnacle of release before they fell into each other's arms, bodies pressed into one another as though they were never going to let go.

Heat emanated from every pore as she felt Fergus all around her, inside her. Fergus. Unbelievable. It was as though she'd found her way home. She couldn't wish for anything else. Her body was so relaxed it felt impossible to move. Her head was filled with wonder, and her heart beat to a rhythm of happiness. Fergus.

Holding Tamara as though he'd never let go, Fergus closed his eyes and let the moment take over. His body had no strength left. He'd poured everything into her. He'd lost all sense of anything else but Tamara. He couldn't believe how wonderful she'd felt in his arms. Her body so receptive to his. She'd given herself to him without hesitation. As he'd given back to her, hopefully making her feel just as wonderful. It felt as though this was always meant to happen and finally they'd got there. Who'd have thought their lovemaking would be so intense? That they'd be so in sync? Instinctively she'd understood his needs. He might've wanted to have sex with her in the past, but not once had he imagined how amazing it would be. He'd been unwilling to revisit those feelings after learning Tamara would be in Vanuatu with him, sceptical that he might be hanging on to something that had never really existed. So life could still surprise him, make him feel great. Were there more surprises to come?

'Hey, are you awake?' she asked quietly.

'Wide awake. Though I doubt my body is up to moving at all right at the moment. I'm whacked.'

'Me too. It's been quite a day after a frightening night.' Then she chuckled. 'Which has nothing to do with how I feel right now. All soft and warm and cosy. And happy to be with you.'

He'd take that any time. Brushing a kiss on the top of her head, he said, 'If the earthquakes are still bothering you, you could catch a flight home when they're available.' He wouldn't blame her if she did, but he'd be disappointed now that they'd reached this stage in their wobbly relationship. They'd only just got to know each other intimately, and it was nowhere near enough. Having made love, he hoped the wobble was gone and they'd get on better than ever. There was potential for their so-called friendship to grow into something more. If he wanted that. If Tamara wanted that. His gut clenched. He had no idea what she thought. But neither did she know how he felt about her. Because he wasn't at all certain himself, yet. There was still a long way to go. But in the meantime, he'd make the most of being this close to her.

Up on her elbows, Tamara smiled down at him. 'No way. I came to do a job and I'll see it to the finish.' Her smile widened. 'Not to mention how we've started something I'd like to keep on with.'

'Phew. You know how to make me feel good.'

'You weren't doubting my enjoyment, were you?' By the sudden tight look on her face, it was a serious question. 'Because if you were, let me tell you that I want more as soon as I've recovered and had a shower.'

Was that her way of saying all was good? He wasn't sure, but he wasn't going to stir up trouble by asking. 'Throw in a meal and you've got me.' She already had him, but it didn't hurt to play hard to get just a little.

Slowly the smile returned. 'Let's go, then. I'm starving.'

She'd said that often over the past two weeks. 'When aren't you?'

'When I'm making out with you.'

'That's better.' Way better. He'd take that anytime and oblige in making her happy—and satisfied.

Crawling off the bed, Tamara looked around the room. 'Oh cripes. We didn't close the curtains.'

His gut tossed up a deep laugh. 'Just as well the sun went down over an hour ago.'

'Plus we didn't switch on any lights.' Her grin struck him hard.

Tamara was beautiful. He couldn't get enough of her. Knowing that amazing body better, he hoped there'd be a lot more to come. 'Go have a shower while I close us in and straighten the bed.'

She wiggled her delectable backside at him. 'You could always join me.'

'I could, but then we wouldn't make it to dinner, and right now I know I have to eat or I'll lose it.'

'You get hangry?'

'I do.'

'Then I'll get that shower.'

Watching her walk to the bathroom while remaining where he stood turned out to be the hardest thing he'd done all day. He only managed because he promised himself they'd get together, up close and sexy again later. Life hadn't looked this good in forever.

CHAPTER NINE

'LIZ, I NEED to examine you internally,' Fergus told the woman writhing in pain on the bed.

'No problem, Doc. I know what goes on. This isn't my first baby. But my daughter was born at full term, not several weeks early.'

Fear and tension due to the quake might've brought on contractions. 'When did you feel the first contraction?' Tamara asked.

'About an hour after the earthquake.'

Tamara reached for Liz's hand. 'You're like me? You were scared out of your mind?'

'You bet I was. I'd never been in one before. They're not common in Australia.'

'I was in a big one thirteen years ago and I still freaked out on Friday.'

Tamara felt the shudder that wracked Liz and fully understood what had brought it on. If she hadn't had Fergus there, she wouldn't have been feeling as relaxed. Add in all the lovemaking they'd got up to in the days and nights since the quake and relaxed was an understatement. Fergus was wonderful. He'd shown no signs of thinking she wasn't good enough in bed. In fact, he'd been vocally enthusiastic! But it was early days for sure, and she wasn't going to ruin everything by overthinking his reactions. Instead, she'd make the most of his exceptional lovemaking and leave the future alone for now.

He crouched down at the end of the bed. 'Liz, can you part your legs?'

As Liz did so, she looked to Tamara. 'Fun being a woman, isn't it?'

'Men have no idea how lucky they are.'

'How far along did you say you are?' Fergus asked.

'Thirty weeks.'

'Any chance you're out by a few weeks?'

'I suppose it's possible. I wasn't very regular. Why?'

'I think baby's bigger than I'd expect for thirty weeks.'

'That's got to be good news, isn't it?'

'Definitely. Every week helps.' Fergus stood up. 'But I also have to tell you that baby's stuck in the wrong position. As I can't move him or her, it means doing a caesarean.'

Tamara reached for Liz's hand. 'You'll get through this, Liz. You've got a superb surgeon on your side.'

Fergus's eyes widened briefly, and he smiled at her.

Liz was staring at Fergus as though he'd grown horns. 'You're serious?'

Fergus nodded. 'Unfortunately, I can't change what's going on. There could be further complications if I don't go in and retrieve the baby. I wouldn't do a caesarean if I didn't believe it was essential.'

Blunt, but it worked.

Liz sagged. 'Do whatever you have to, to save my baby.'

'Do you want me to go and find your cousin?' Tamara asked her. Liz needed someone close with her at the moment.

'Please. Tell her to try and get in touch with Jay.'

Glancing at Fergus as she headed out of the room, Tamara bit her lip. Would he leave her side if she was having their baby? After his actions during and following the earthquake, she thought he wouldn't.

What the heck? She shouldn't even be thinking that. Far too soon! More likely they'd never reach that point. She might be enjoying his lovemaking, but caution still prevailed about falling in love with him. Not because she and Fergus once hadn't got along, but because of how her ex had treated her, lying and cheating and blaming it all on her. She'd believed she'd come to terms with what he'd done, but now she was sleeping with Fergus, so content in his arms each night, the wariness was suddenly returning in full force. She had to take this one day at a time and not rush anything.

'Tamara, I want you in Theatre with me,' was the first thing Fergus said when she returned to the cubicle with Liz's relative in tow.

'Glad to help.' She needed something good happening to take the edge off the many hours they were putting in here.

'Thought you might be.' Fergus smiled. 'I'm going to find an anaesthetist and organise a bed in Theatre. Stay with Liz until I'm ready. She's more upset than she's letting on.'

'No surprise. She's determined to be strong, but not having her husband here makes it hard.'

'We're going to name him Fergus,' Liz's husband said later as he sat beside the crib where his son lay attached to monitors and an oxygen mask.

Fergus's face reddened. 'You don't have to do that.'

'Maybe not, but we're going to anyway.' Liz looked exhausted, but her face was alight with love. 'Don't think Fergus Tamara really works, though.'

Tamara burst out laughing. 'I couldn't agree more.' Though she might be happy to tie her name with Fergus's surname one day, if she could get over the panic that had set in earlier. Sure, it was fading a little now, but it had been a wake-up call, for sure. Her emotions were all over the place, one moment wanting to trust her heart and let loose, the next wanting to hunker down and hide. So far, there was no reason to doubt him. He'd changed so much it was exciting getting to know this new version. He still looked the world in the eye, but the arrogance was nowhere to be seen. He was kind and caring with his patients and other people he spent time with. There were so many things about him that warmed her and made her wonder if at last she truly had found the man she'd been looking for most of her adult life. But John had caused so much damage with his lies and cheating. Did she really know Fergus well enough yet to trust him with her fragile heart?

'Feel like going along the road for a meal?' Fergus asked Tamara when they'd finished up for the day.

'I'd prefer to go back to the resort and stroll along the beach, maybe take a dip in the pool before having dinner, if that's okay with you.'

'The resort it is.' They'd been lucky. People had been cancelling their holidays since the earthquake so there were rooms going begging all over the island. He wanted to pay for their room, but the owner wasn't listening to him, merely said he was pleased to have them there. It gave him something to do, he'd said with a cheeky smile.

'We're keeping the cook happy too. She likes preparing meals.'

'I don't eat that much,' Tamara joked as he drove away from the hospital.

'Want to bet?' For someone so slim, she managed to put away a fair amount of food. 'Where do you put it all?' That svelte body turned him on with only a glance. 'It doesn't show at all.'

'It's in the genes. My dad was lean, and Mum wasn't big either.' She eyed him up and down. 'I'd say you got your father's genes. Tall, slight without being skinny, and muscular.'

'Mum's tall and slim,' he said quickly, wanting nothing to do with his father. 'She has to work hard at keeping her weight in check, though.' He'd sort of admitted he was like his father. Only physically, but memories of his so-called mates saying he was going to turn out a con artist like his old man were never far away.

'I remember her being beautifully dressed whenever she came to watch you play rugby.'

'You were at most of those games, weren't you?' he asked, aiming to shift the direction of the conversation away from his parents.

'All the girls were. What better way to spend a Saturday morning than watching the hunky college boys playing rugby in their tight-fitting T-shirts and shorts?' Her grin was huge. 'Those were the days. All innocence and fun.' The grin dimmed a little. 'Mostly.'

'For us lads, it was watching you girls in shorts that accentuated your legs while playing netball that wound us up.' Hopefully that wouldn't give her a reason to bring up the subject of him being rude to her.

Thankfully, Tamara laughed. 'Typical teens. Something about those days was kind of carefree. We knew there was a lot ahead in terms of studying and getting serious about being adults and were probably postponing it by having a lot of fun.'

'You've nailed it.' Parking outside the resort, he turned to her. 'I am glad we've caught up again. I've always regretted what happened between us. We're getting on better than I'd ever believed possible.' He hauled in a lungful of air. 'I'm really enjoying spending time with you, Tamara. You're one amazing lady.'

She stared at him wide-eyed.

Had he shocked her with his honesty? Did she still have doubts about how much he'd changed? Please not that. 'I mean it.'

'I know you do.'

'But?'

'But nothing.' She leaned over and planted a kiss on his mouth, then locked her eyes with his. 'I feel the same as you. Spending time together here has been great, and I'm looking forward to more.'

Hauling her into his arms, he kissed her like

his life depended upon it. Which, right at this moment, it seemed like it did. 'We're on the same page,' he whispered before plunging his tongue back inside her mouth, sending need spiralling throughout his body. 'Now let's get on the same bed.'

Fergus woke to loud knocking on the door. 'Why? Who?' He wanted to stay snuggled up to Tamara for another hour or so. Hauling himself out of bed, he wrapped a towel around his waist and opened the door to find Tim about to knock again. 'Morning.' Through the broken windows in the hall, he could see the sun rising over the hill.

'We're needed for an urgent operation. Twelve-year-old boy rode his four-wheel motorbike into a five-metre hole during the night.'

That would've caused serious injuries. 'What about the girls?'

Tim shook his head. 'Leave them sleeping. There are nurses preparing for us right now. I'll warm up the ute.' The vehicle they'd been lent since the van couldn't get through all the potholes on the road from here to the hospital.

'Be right with you.'

Throwing on shorts and a T-shirt, Fergus leaned down to brush a light kiss on Tamara's cheek. 'See you later,' he whispered.

She didn't stir. Showed how exhausted she was

coping with the after-effects of the quake. As they all were. It would be too easy to slip back under the sheet with her, but at the moment he needed to tug on his doctor hat.

What had the kid been doing riding in the dark with all the damage out there? He should've been at home with his family. Not his problem. Putting the kid back together was his concern. He said to Tim, 'I take it I'm the lackey for this op.' It didn't bother him. They'd worked together a couple of times over the days since the quake, as there weren't many cases turning up that he specialised in. He was upping his basic surgical skills working with Tim. Never hurt to learn more.

Tim grinned. 'You bet. It's a boy we're operating on, remember?'

Fergus laughed. 'True.' He did enjoy Tim's company. The guy took his work seriously but could still have fun, which always helped when the case was serious. He enjoyed working with Tamara too. Not only because she was very competent and obviously got a lot from her work, but because occasionally she'd give him one of those heart-warming smiles that moved him deeply. Of course, the smiles were reflected in her gorgeous aqua eyes, and although he couldn't see those lips he enjoyed kissing because of the mask she wore, he knew what her mouth looked like. Yes, he was starting to think he might have it bad.

'You and Tamara are still getting on well,' Tim observed as he turned into the hospital grounds.

'We are.' *Leave it at that, mate.* It was far too soon to talk about how he felt or what he hoped for—if he ever opened up to anyone, which was unlikely. He hadn't been good at talking to others about his feelings since being jeered at about his father.

'I'll shut up about now,' Tim said as he parked.

'Good idea.' Fergus chuckled. Tim would do exactly that. From the times he'd spent with him he'd come to understand he wasn't one for stirring up trouble. 'Let's get this underway.'

As he scrubbed up, he spent a brief moment thinking about Tamara. Again. Seeing her lying curled up in the bed they'd thoroughly messed up making love before falling asleep in each other's arms. She was coming to mean so much to him, which was a worry. He wasn't sure he could easily hand over his heart again after what Harriet had done to him. If he didn't take risks, he had nothing to look forward to—but it was such a huge, frightening step.

'You ready?' Tim called from the doorway.

'As ready as I'll ever be.' For work, if not love. He headed to Theatre. Time to get on with practicalities.

Tamara sat on the sofa, her legs tucked under her backside. 'I keep thinking about those kids racing around playing hide-and-seek and causing their mothers never-ending worry over the danger they might get into around the wrecked buildings.' They'd spent the day visiting small villages to offer aid.

Fergus placed a very full glass of wine on the small table at her elbow. 'I think it's the kids' way of coping with what's happened. They're terrified whenever there's an aftershock and get busy running away to hide.'

'At least the aftershocks have slowed down and aren't as strong.' She'd slept uninterrupted for four hours last night, before waking up—not to a quake, but to the absence of one. The quakes, along with the long hours they were working, had screwed with her mind to the point that she wasn't always sure where she was whenever she woke from a deep sleep.

'To think we're leaving here in two days' time. Home and comfortable while these people will still be struggling to get through each day.' Fergus took a mouthful of beer. 'I considered staying on, even though I have commitments back home. I talked to Kaikea, but he believes they have things under control and, if anything, he'd prefer I returned next year to continue the work I've been doing.'

'Do you think you will?' She knew she would—if they promised no earthquakes.

'I'd like to, but I've already told the volunteer

service that I'd go where they needed next year. A second stint back here, away from my practice, would be asking a lot of my partners.'

'Didn't you say you're on the North Shore?'

He nodded. 'I never thought I'd move to Auckland once I'd qualified. It makes Nelson feel like a suburb. A beautiful one, though.'

'And friendly. It's a rare time I don't bump into someone I know when I walk down Trafalgar Street.'

'Know what you mean,' Fergus muttered darkly.

She'd clearly touched a sore point. He probably got bad-mouthed by people, but it was quite the opposite for her. 'I wasn't referring to things you'd prefer left alone.'

'It's all right, Tamara. It's over and done with.'

Except it wasn't. She could see the hurt and anger in his expression. He hadn't done anything wrong. He hadn't been the guilty party. She stood up and crossed to wrap her arms around his tense body. 'I am sorry.' She truly was. He'd changed so much that he deserved to be recognised for who he'd become and not the teen of the past. Another squeeze and she returned to the sofa.

He remained silent, but his back wasn't quite so tight and those delectable lips no longer looked grim.

Sipping wine, she stared out at the pool with

the palm trees on the far side. Enticing, if it didn't take energy to get up and go change into her bikini before jumping in. Far easier to stay put, enjoying the company. Despite that little setback, she was relaxed with Fergus pretty much all the time now. Sometimes she had to pinch herself in case she was dreaming and about to wake up to find he wasn't half as wonderful as she believed. He listened whenever she talked about anything—as her father used to. Her ex never took the time to hear what she had to say about most things. And he'd thought she was cold. But she hadn't even told Fergus that she'd once been married, not wanting memories of John to taint her time here. Did it matter? It probably did if she wanted this to go anywhere.

'I checked out the zip line but it's closed. Not sure if it was damaged or the owners are being cautious. Whatever the reason I'm disappointed.' Now he was smiling. 'That was an awesome thing to do, and something I'll do more often in other places.'

'Count me in.'

Plonking himself down on the chair opposite her, he laughed. 'Have to find one that's handy. They don't pop up all over the place.'

'Shouldn't be too hard. There's one in Kaikoura. It'd be an overnight trip from Nelson.'

Nothing wrong with that if they were sharing a room and a bed.

His smile backed off a little. ‘I don’t often go down to Nelson for longer than one or two nights.’

Of course he didn’t. ‘Fair enough.’

‘I try to see my grandparents regularly, but I don’t usually allow time to do anything else.’

‘Where’s the retirement village they’ve moved to?’

‘In Bishopdale, on the hill overlooking Tahunanui and Tasman Bay. Grandad’s got osteoarthritis and looking after the grounds and the house got too much for him.’

A very expensive place too. Guess they hadn’t been fooled into investing their money with their son. ‘It’s a lovely place.’

‘They find it strange being contained—Grandma’s word, not mine—in a small unit and not having to worry about a thing, but it’s good they don’t have to mow lawns or maintain the house they used to have.’

‘You’ll stay with them at Christmas?’

‘Yes.’ He hesitated, as if wondering how to say whatever was on his mind.

She waited, not wanting to interrupt in case he reacted badly. She still didn’t know him well enough to read his mind.

‘The other day I mentioned us getting together

at some point.' He could've sounded more enthusiastic.

'I'll be disappointed if we didn't. I'll text you my address. Drop in any time you like, other than Christmas Day, when I'll be at Sashi's.'

'Will do.'

As easy as that? He didn't seem to get that she understood his problems and wouldn't try to make things more difficult. Hopefully, he'd start to see that soon and let go of his hang-ups. 'Good.' She wouldn't overplay her enthusiasm even when he'd shaken her about how well they were getting on. Could it be she was putting more into what they had going than he was? At the end of the day, they were just having a fling while they were both on this island. A fling she'd hoped might eventually grow into something deeper. But Fergus perhaps didn't see it that way. There could even be someone back in Auckland he spent time with. She'd never asked.

Tamara's heart sank. She'd been rushing in blindly, believing this Fergus was so unlike the old one that she could accept the feelings she'd once had for him were real and this time there'd be nothing getting in the way of them. Or she could just be overreacting and needed to get a grip on her emotions. Just because it had been a while since she'd felt this way about someone, it didn't mean she was fully ready to trust again. Not so quickly, anyway.

‘Want a top-up?’ Fergus asked, nodding at her nearly empty glass.

Why not? She wasn’t working for the next twelve hours. ‘Please.’

‘I hear that the Last Resort Café has opened up again. Would you like to go there for a meal tonight? It would be a change, and good to support them.’

They were supporting the owner of this resort now that he’d finally given in and had accepted that they pay for their food and drinks at least. But Fergus was right. They did spend all their time at the hospital or in this bungalow, so a change would be good. ‘Great idea.’

The relief in Fergus’s face suggested he wanted to get away from here because it was almost too cosy. Another warning he wasn’t as keen as she was for this fling to go somewhere.

Placing the wine on the table, he looked at her. ‘Bet you’re looking forward to catching up with your family again.’

‘I am. Especially Sashi’s little guys.’ She couldn’t wait to see their faces when they saw the trampoline she’d bought them for Christmas.

‘Kids, eh? They twist your heart when you’re not looking.’

She gulped. Fergus had said that? To her? ‘They sure do. I adore the boys. They’re a great pick-me-up on the down days. But I don’t have to be there for them twenty-four seven. Not that it would be a problem if I was. After how Dad looked after us all the time we were growing up, it's the only way I know how to be with children.'

'Is Sashi the same?'

'Absolutely. Sometimes she worries something bad might happen, that she won't be there to see them grow up, and goes overboard caring for them.'

'Better that than not at all.'

'I agree. I'll be the same if I'm ever lucky enough to have children.' It was her turn to say too much, but then wasn't that part of getting to know each other better?

'You'd like a family?'

'Of course.'

Fergus drained his beer quickly and stood up. Closing down that subject before they got too deep? Her heart twisted.

'Let's make a move and get to the café before it fills up. Many tourists who can't get off the island are bored silly and spending a lot of time in the bars and restaurants that have reopened,' he said.

'Shall I ring and make a booking?'

'I'll own up. I already did that in the hope you'd agree to go with me.'

'Why wouldn't I?' They were sleeping together, sharing meals here and having a drink, if not revealing everything about themselves.

He shrugged. 'I'm still reluctant to readily accept that we're at the stage where I can go ahead and make a plan without talking to you first.'

'Fergus Collier. The past is exactly that. I do not look for the arrogant young guy I once knew. He's gone. Not completely, because that's impossible, and I wouldn't want everything about you to be different, but I like who you've become. A lot. Now I'm going to change my shorts for a skirt. Back in a moment.' She strode into the bedroom without looking at him. She'd said her piece and didn't want to hear any more about the subject.

With a rare warmth in his chest, Fergus watched Tamara charge into the bedroom. She knew how to wake him up while putting him in his place at the same time. She was the first, apart from his grandparents, to acknowledge he'd truly changed. It was as though the attraction that flickered between them when they were young had flared up bigger and brighter, making him see her for real. As Tamara appeared to be seeing him. Was there a future for them? One where they had those children she'd mentioned and obviously longed for? One where he could believe he was genuinely loved for who he was?

Accepting she liked him enough to spend most of her free time with him didn't come easily. A lot of which was in bed or at a table eating. Nothing to complain about there, but she'd just told him she liked the man he'd become. No wonder his heart was out of sync. It didn't have a clue what was going on.

She'd noticed how worried he'd been when he'd thought she was talking about his past and had been quick to reassure him she wasn't. He shouldn't have worried in the first place. It was a long-held habit, but he needed to trust her not to say things aimed at hurting him. If only memories of what Harriet had done didn't keep raising their heads. *She'd* sworn it didn't bother her about his father's crimes, that it was Fergus she loved and therefore had no issues with his past. Then she'd changed her mind.

Which was why he struggled to trust Tamara, even when she was aware of what had happened. She had tried to see the true picture. Yet she'd also had every reason to rub it in and mock him. But she hadn't. Something he'd been grateful for and kept tucked away in his head to take out and smile about whenever the going got too rough. In the beginning that was often. Despite that, his heart wasn't an object to hand around willy nilly. At the moment, he was in two minds over whether to toss caution to the wind and take a risk on finding out if they were meant to be together, or to remain locked down and safe.

Safe sounded boring. It *was* boring. He loved

how he and Tamara were in bed. How she smiled at him as though he'd given her a gift every time they made love. How she curled in against him, seemingly without a care in the world. At least he hoped she wasn't wondering if he might hurt her in some way. That was the last thing he wanted, but it was difficult to be completely open and honest with her. Another bad habit, but one that had kept his emotions safe whenever he'd caught up with someone from the past. He also realised he still knew very little about what she'd done in the years since he'd last seen her, other than her nursing career, and losing her dad. She'd been just as close-mouthed about her romantic past as he had, but surely she had one. Didn't that signal a fundamental lack of trust between them?

Tamara skipped into the room. 'Ready as I'll ever be.'

Okay, this wasn't the time to be gloomy or question everything. He liked being with Tamara and, at the moment, that's what mattered. 'You look lovely.' Good enough to wrap up in his arms and carry her to the bedroom. He'd have to wait. They had a date first. Catching her hand, he let them out the door. 'Let's party.'

She beamed from ear to ear. 'Bring it on.'

They would enjoy wining and dining and for a couple of hours pretend everything was right with Vanuatu. Then they could return to their room and definitely wind up the tempo.

* * *

The restaurant was full to overflowing. 'Just as well you made a reservation,' Tamara said. 'Otherwise, we'd be going hungry.'

'We still might have to wait a while, but at least the wine won't need any working on.' Fergus nodded for her to follow the waitress to a table in a corner.

'I overheard what you said. The cooks are keeping up with the orders so not a long wait. Can I get that wine you mentioned right away?' the waitress asked.

Fergus nodded. 'Please. Tamara? What would you like?'

'Chardonnay, thanks.' It was the one wine they both liked. Slipping onto the chair he'd pulled out, she gave him a smile. She could get used to this.

Sitting opposite, he looked around before focusing on her. 'I'll miss this place. The time's gone quite fast, despite the earthquake.'

It was hard to believe she'd soon be back in Nelson catching up with Sashi and her family. Fergus had said he'd be in town for Christmas and that they should catch up. Hopefully, he meant it. 'I can't believe it, either. But then it's been tricky keeping track of hours and days with all that's been going on.'

The waitress arrived with the wine, two glasses,

and menus. 'The menu's rather limited, but it's the best we can manage at the moment.'

'We're just happy to eat,' Tamara told her. 'And not have to cook,' she added. Something that wasn't her favourite pastime. She was okay at putting a meal together but no chef. Noting what Fergus liked to eat, she believed he had a taste for high-end food, not the everyday stews or chops she cooked.

'Glad you understand. Not everyone's as easy to please. But then, aren't you two working in the hospital?'

'We are,' she said. Was there anyone on the island who didn't know who they were?

'The other doctor with you helped my brother after the quake. He broke a leg falling off the balcony of his house.'

'How's he doing now?' Fergus asked.

'Apart from having to sit around and do nothing, he's fine.' The waitress smiled. 'In other words, grumpy as can be. I'll be back shortly for your orders.'

She was right. There wasn't a lot on offer. Tamara quickly decided on steak with whatever vegetables were available.

'Same for me.' Fergus placed his menu on the table and lifted his glass of wine to tap hers. 'To a quieter last couple of days.'

She tapped back. 'Agreed.' Yet a sense of finality was creeping in, and she couldn't put her finger on what was causing it. Did she ask Fergus whether he'd like to see more of her once they were home? Or did she sit back and enjoy dinner and leave tricky subjects alone? That was probably the easier option. No doubt the wisest. But she didn't always do wise. After taking a sip of wine, she placed the glass on the table and began twisting it back and forth between her fingers.

'What are you thinking?' Fergus asked.

'About life once we're back home.'

'Ahh. I see.'

Did he though? 'We will stay in touch, won't we? I want to.'

'Of course we will.' He reached for her free hand. 'I don't want to never see you again after we leave here.'

Meaning? That he wanted to see her a lot? Or just catch up whenever it fitted into his busy life?

'What would you both like to order?' The waitress was back.

'Medium rare steak, and the vegetables,' Tamara told her.

'Same for me,' Fergus answered, still focused on her.

'We live a long way apart,' she pointed out as the waitress disappeared.

Fergus leaned back in his chair. 'Less than an hour and a half by plane.'

'And almost that long to drive from the airport to your part of the city,' she said, but she felt a crushing sense of relief. So, this wasn't the end of everything. There was more to come. What that turned out to be was still to be worked through, but she'd go with the flow. After taking a mouthful of wine, she set the glass down. As long as she could stop worrying, she'd be happy. More wine might help there.

After dinner, they strolled barefoot along the beach, hand in hand. The closer to the far end they got, the more concerns about Fergus and what he might want from her began to rise again. So much for being happy. She was still tense. On edge. Nothing new there, after how John made her feel when he left. He hadn't ever liked her honesty; said she could be brutal when she wanted to know something. But for her it was the only way she knew how to be. She'd learned that when her mother died and friends of her parents began tiptoeing around her. She wanted them to be normal, not strange. She'd hoped being open and honest would resolve that. It didn't work with everyone, but it was her way.

So, here went nothing. 'Do you have someone special in your life back home?'

Fergus came to an abrupt halt. He dropped her hand as though it was on fire and turned to look at her with incredulous eyes that hardened as she watched. 'No, I do not,' he snapped. 'Do you think I'd have slept with you if I did?'

She'd gone too far. 'Not really. I'm sorry, but I like to know exactly where I stand with the men I date.'

'Subtlety was never your strong point, was it?' He wasn't calming down.

While she was starting to get wound up. 'I prefer to call it being frank.'

'I'm sure you do.' He began striding back the way they'd come.

She kept pace with him. 'Fergus, I'm sorry, but I wasn't looking for trouble. I wanted to be certain you were totally single, that's all.'

'Yes, Tamara, I am, and I'm likely to stay that way. I've been engaged before, and that was a fail; wc never made it to the altar. Not something I'd like to repeat. Okay?'

No. Not at all. 'I've been married. It was so awful when it fell apart that I thought I'd never want to fall in love again. But now, four years on, I would like to try again, if I can put what happened behind me, which isn't as easy as I'd hoped.'

He spun around to stare at her again. 'You never mentioned being married. Why tell me now?'

'I'm being honest and hoping to get closer to you by opening up.' Right now, it looked like that was never happening. 'To show you that you can talk to me even when you're reluctant to talk about the past. I have to admit, I've wondered what else you don't want to talk about. Why didn't you tell me about your fiancée?'

'You want me to haul myself through all my past troubles again when I've finally managed to bury them.' Not a question, but a statement. 'Forget it. I'm not going there for anything or anyone.'

'If we're going to be in any kind of a relationship, then we need to talk about things that came between us, and other things that have happened to each of us since we last saw each other.' She was prepared to talk about why her marriage failed, explain how John had hurt her saying she was cold and unloving, and blaming her for his lies and cheating.

He was staring at her as though he wanted to see right inside her. 'Tamara, it's only been two weeks since we started sleeping together. I don't call that a relationship or anywhere near one.'

'Is that why you clammed up when I mentioned your father earlier?'

'Yes, damn it, it was. You know what happened, so there's no reason to talk about it.'

'I think there is. I'm not looking to cause trouble or stir things up for you. I want you to understand how much I care about you. How I admire you for working your way through all the backlash and coming out whole.' She mightn't have gone running to his side to help at the time, but he'd have shoved her away if she had. Anyway, she hadn't. Instead, she'd wished him well but never told him so. 'Partners should support one another.'

'So I thought until my fiancée proved otherwise.' He began walking again, slower this time but still with a determined step. 'Don't bother asking what happened. I'm not talking about that either. Neither am I asking what went wrong with your marriage.'

Then this was the end of the road for them. There could be no relationship of any kind if he refused to open up, to show her his vulnerabilities, to take the risk and try to love her. Tamara gritted her teeth. She might've been called cold and uncaring by John, but she did truly care about Fergus and what happened to him. There was a warmth within her that had risen as she got to know him since arriving in Port Vila. A warmth that made her feel whole again and rekindled her need to love and be loved. A warmth that now seemed to be fading. She did want to share her heart with Fergus, but only if they could talk about anything and everything. Trust one another fully. 'What's really eating at you? What's wrong with asking for the truth?'

'Like I said, I've done that once and it cost me everything. I lost the woman I loved, who I believed I'd be spending the rest of my life with. I am not prepared to go through that again.'

'We're on the same page there. But for different reasons.' If she understood him correctly. 'Having said that, I might be willing to try again if I met the right man.' *I have, but it seems he doesn't want the role.* In fact, he didn't seem particularly interested in the fact she'd once been married or why she was now single again. So, he could go take a leap. For them to go forward together, they had to at least listen to each other!

'I wish you all the best, Tamara. I really do.' He remained silent until they reached the ute, which he unlocked, then held open her door. 'Maybe we were never meant to be more than a brief fling. It didn't work out between us the first time and I did want to get to know you, then. This time, we've got on great, but there are problems that we can't ignore. I don't trust any woman not to let me down, and from what I'm hearing, I doubt you trust any man not to walk out on you again, either. Let's face it; it's not a recipe for success, is it?' He closed the door and walked around to the driver's side.

There was nothing to say about that. Fergus was right. She had struggled badly with trust issues, had wondered if she'd ever truly, fully be able to fall in love again. She knew she'd been falling deeper and deeper for Fergus every day, but did she trust him not to walk away without a backward glance when it wasn't working for him? She wasn't sure. And if she wasn't sure, then she had no right to insist he give her a chance.

* * *

So much for a hot, sexy night of lovemaking after dinner. Fergus removed his clothes from the bedroom they'd been sharing. The couch was his for the remaining two nights. He couldn't lie beside Tamara and not reach for her, and that would be what he'd do when her scent filled the air around him and the heat from her body drifted his way.

He was a fool. He should've talked to her about his feelings regarding his father—and his mother—and got them out of the way. And he should have told her about Harriet, although the fact that she'd kept her own marriage a secret was a concern too.

Tamara was right; partners should stand by one another. If he wanted more time getting closer to her, then it was the only way to go. But what if, like Harriet, Tamara ultimately decided he wasn't worth the risk? Didn't want to be Mrs Collier? Didn't want to have his children, who might be tainted by his family name? He wanted to accept that just because Harriet had walked away from him, Tamara wouldn't, but it was beyond him. There'd been one too many knockbacks in his life to be able to accept a person into his life so easily. Even someone who'd known him for so long.

He couldn't deny Tamara got to him in unexpected ways. She always had, if he thought about it, which was why they'd always pressed each other's buttons back then.

Here in Port Vila, she'd tripped every button in his body, and in his head, in completely different ways. He wanted her even more than he'd wanted Harriet, and that was what totally scared the pants off him. Making him run from a chance of love, turning him into a coward.

'Goodnight, Fergus.' Tamara stood in the bedroom doorway, watching him with a guarded look on her face.

It would be so easy to walk across and haul her into his arms, hold her, kiss her, make love to her until all the pain disappeared. But that wouldn't solve a thing. There were some serious problems standing between them. Ones he was afraid to push through in case there was no happy-ever-after waiting for them on the other side. 'Goodnight, Tamara.'

The door shut with a bang. As did his heart. Time to toughen up and get on with his real life. One with no dreams of the impossible. It was far safer all round.

Stretching out on the couch with his legs hanging over the end, hands behind his head, he stared up at the fan rotating above. There'd be no sleep for him tonight.

'Bring him round, Ian.' Fergus stepped back from the operating table after opening and cleaning wounds made by rusty nails in the boy's thigh.

The kid had been playing in a shed that had

partially collapsed after the quake and had fallen onto a board with nails sticking out. Six years old and very fidgety, Fergus had preferred to put the lad under for the time it took to clean and stitch the wounds rather than use a local anaesthetic.

Tamara wiped the last of the blood from the boy's thigh and tossed the swabs in the bin. She looked tired, as though she hadn't had any more sleep over the last forty-eight hours than he had. 'I'll stay with him,' she said quietly.

No chirpiness in her voice today. Nor yesterday as they'd worked side by side. 'He won't take long to come round and will probably be in a hurry to get out of here and see what his friends are up to.'

She nodded. 'He's an energetic wee guy.'

At least they still agreed on some things. 'Our next patient is a man with appendicitis.'

'You did appendectomies during your training?'

'Yes.' Otherwise, he wouldn't be doing this one. But Tamara would know that and was probably only making conversation, as it was awfully quiet between them most of the time. 'I've already explained to Kaikea that I haven't done one in years, but he says it's urgent and another doctor won't be available for a long while.'

'Makes sense. I feel for the other women we came to help who didn't get their operations because of the quake.'

'Me too.' Who knew when they'd get help

now? He might make an exception about doing two trips in one year, or tell the volunteer committee that he wanted to return here to finish that list.

Tamara looked thoughtful. 'I'll come back if there's someone available to do the surgeries.' She didn't lock eyes on him.

His gut sank. They were in a mess. But he made up his mind about one thing bothering him. 'I'm definitely going to volunteer to come back.' Did that mean they'd be a team again? Could he manage that after all that had happened? What was more important? His heart or helping those in need?

Tamara's mouth flattened as she pushed the bed up to the table. What did that mean? She didn't want to work with him anymore?

He couldn't blame her. He'd shut down on her when she'd mentioned her marriage and had flung the news about Harriet at her, without properly explaining that disaster, either. She'd have suffered when her marriage broke down. No way she wouldn't have done. This was Tamara. She gave her all when she was involved with other people, and he doubted she'd be any different when it came to a partner. And while they'd managed to work together efficiently, there had been uncomfortable moments which, on reflection, he now realised showed him that she didn't trust him easily. Now hurt and anger hung between them, and there was no way to fix it without opening up completely, something he'd struggle to do. But he would tell her what he planned to do here. 'I can't leave those women wondering what's going to happen now that I've met them. It's not in me to do that.'

'I know.'

Knock his socks off. She hadn't let their break-up get in the way of that. Why couldn't he be the same? Say what was on his mind, see how she reacted and learn how she felt about him? If only it was that simple. *It could be, if you truly want to find happiness.*

There was the problem. He'd realised he did want love. Without all the fears, without looking over his shoulder waiting for the axe to fall. It was hard to believe Tamara would do something awful to hurt him. But. There was always a huge *but* holding him back. Would he ever be free of it?

CHAPTER TEN

STANDING AT THE luggage carousel in Auckland International Airport, Tamara shivered. It might be summer here, but it was a lot cooler than Vanuatu. It wasn't the weather making her shiver though. It was Fergus. This was the last time she'd see him, and that hurt beyond anything she'd imagined. As bad as when her marriage had ended.

No, worse. She and Fergus hadn't cleared the air between them. Fergus had remained withdrawn from her since the night he'd refused to talk about himself and had ended their fling. She hadn't been any better, though, because she'd believed he wouldn't want to know about John and her trust issues.

'Your bag?' Fergus pointed to the carousel.

'Looks like it.' She stepped forward to grab it off the conveyor belt but Fergus beat her to it.

'I've got it.' He swung it up and placed it beside her, then reached for another one. 'Guess that's it then. I'll catch a cab and get back to reality.'

Reality? She couldn't even imagine what that was anymore. Her life had been turned upside down and inside out since Fergus came back into her life. 'I'll walk out with you.' Her flight to Nelson was two hours away, so she'd walk across to the domestic terminal to stretch her legs. The problem being, she wasn't ready to say goodbye to Fergus. Never would be. If only she knew what to say that might have him giving her a chance to talk and tell him what he'd come to mean to her. Could she tell him he held her heart in his hand? If she could be certain he'd listen, then yes, she'd take that risk.

Outside the sun was low in the sky and the air was still. Night-time was approaching. Taxis were lined up at every vacant spot, and people were bustling in all directions. Her heart was heavy. Her head in a spin.

Fergus turned to her. 'Bye, Tamara.' Then he walked away.

Staring after him, she knew she wasn't letting him go that easily. 'Fergus, wait,' she called and ran after him.

He stopped and turned around. 'Yes?'

She paused in front of him. Licked her lips. This wasn't easy. All the things she wanted to say weren't coming out. Her mouth was dry. Her heart pounded as though she'd just run a marathon. 'Fergus—' Sucking in a big breath, she knew she couldn't say what was in her heart. He wouldn't want to hear it. Which would only hurt her. So instead she threw her arms around him and hugged him tight.

His arms lifted slowly, hugged her back, but lightly. It wasn't quite a rejection, more a goodbye.

Pulling back to look at him as her heart began shattering, she said, 'Fergus, you're amazing. I wish you could believe that, and I hope you get everything you want for the future because you truly deserve it.' Placing a light kiss on his chin, she stepped away and headed back to her bag lying on the pavement. Time to get away from here before she fell apart completely.

Stunned, Fergus watched Tamara walk away. She believed in him. She truly did. No one had done that since he was a teen, and even then, he always questioned their motives.

His phone rang. One of his partners at the clinic. 'Hey, Matt, what's up?'

'I'm parked behind the shuttle buses waiting for you.'

'That was close. I was about to grab a taxi. Be right there.' Placing his bag in the boot, he got into the car. 'What brings you all the way over here?'

'Kelvin's in hospital after some fool driving erratically crashed into him on his cycle. His leg's fractured, as are six ribs. Otherwise, he's okay.'

'When did this happen?' Kelvin was injured and nobody had told him?

'Calm down. It only happened three days ago and with everything you've been dealing with in Vanuatu, Kelvin insisted no one tell you till you got back.'

'Of course he did. But I wish you'd ignored him.'

'What could you have done? Swum home to see him?' Matt could do sarcasm as easy as a bird could fly.

'Fair cop. Is he really going to be okay?'

'Yes, though it was a close call. It'll be a while before he's back at work.'

'Just as well the clinic's closed for three weeks.' Oh, yeah, he got it. 'Kelvin's on call for that period.' And Matt was heading to London to see his parents immediately after Christmas. 'I'll be here.' Hopefully, his grandparents would understand he'd have to cut his stay short. What about Tamara? He'd thought he'd stay away from her so as not to raise her hopes, but after what she'd just said to him, he wasn't sure he could remain aloof from her much longer. She was tugging him closer and closer, and he didn't know how he could keep resisting. Or if he even wanted to anymore.

Tamara stared at the self-check-in kiosk. This was it. The final stage of her trip home. The one she didn't want to make because it meant accepting Fergus wasn't going any further with their relationship—the one he'd told her wasn't a relationship. It had been for her, though.

His goodbye had been final. He was never going to open his heart to her. It was too damaged from the past. She had walked away after hugging him. She did know he wanted nothing more to do with her. But— There was always a but!

What if she tried to talk to him once more? She wasn't one to give up easily on something important, and what could be more important than the man who'd stolen her heart? Absolutely nothing. Except to try to win him round would make her seem needy, and as much as she wanted Fergus in her life, she wasn't going to beg. If he wasn't interested, then it would never work out, and she'd be back where she'd started. Heartbroken.

'Do you need help?' an airline assistant asked.

Shaking her head, Tamara looked around and saw the couple standing behind her waiting patiently for her to check in. 'Sorry, I'm thinking about changing my flight plans.' Moving away, she found a row of seats and sat down to consider her options. If she changed her flight without knowing if she could see Fergus, then she might end up forking out for another expensive ticket because the airline wouldn't let her change flights without paying. It would be worth it, though. If

Fergus refused to talk to her, she'd at least know where she stood.

You already know that.

How true. She did. She'd been in denial. Not anymore. Jumping to her feet, she grabbed her bag and joined a queue in front of one of the check-in machines. No more wasting time thinking of ways to get around the pain in her chest. She and Fergus had had a wonderful time and now she had to move on, get her career back on track, forget about love.

Fergus wandered around the house feeling at odds with himself. He usually felt comfortable here. It was his space. No one could throw him off centre. Except tonight it was chilly, as though something—someone?—was missing. Loneliness poured through him. Strange when this was the last place he ever felt that way. Even after an exhausting night working with a patient in labour where everything went wrong, coming home always lifted his spirits. This house was his pride and joy, obtained through his own hard work. No sucking up to strangers to help him obtain his goal. Tonight, though, nothing felt right.

Tamara. She was behind this loneliness. He'd walked away from her at the airport just because he was afraid to lay his heart on the line. Gutless. That's what he was. Now here he was, two hours later, and he was wound up even tighter.

He couldn't accept that he'd let her go when she'd come back to hug him without complaint. He didn't deserve her. Yet he wanted her. So much that the pain was unbearable. What was he going to do? If his heart was broken again at some point in the future, could it be any worse than this?

His phone rang. Hope rose. Tamara? Tugging the phone from his back pocket, he sighed. 'Hi mate. I hear you had a bit of an accident on your bike.'

'That bastard needs to be locked up forever,' Kelvin growled.

'Take it easy,' Fergus muttered. He should've got Matt to drop him off at the hospital to go see Kelvin instead of coming home to feel sorry for himself. 'Matt filled me in on what happened. Just glad you're okay, buddy.'

'Cheers,' he said. 'How'd it go with Tamara?'

If Kelvin wasn't lying in hospital with several broken bones, Fergus would've hung up on him. 'Better than expected.' He could've lied and said she'd been a pain in the butt and he was glad to get away from her, but Kelvin knew him better than that. 'We got along well, really well. But now I'm home and everything's back to normal.' There was a hitch in his voice when he said that.

Sure enough, Kelvin latched onto it straight away. 'You don't understand normal, Fergus. Stop wasting time procrastinating. You've already wasted too much time trying to protect yourself. If Tamara's ringing your bells, then do something about it. You've always had a soft spot for her.'

'You finished?'

'No, but I'm too tired to carry on.'

Fergus tried to laugh. Failed. 'Kelvin.' He paused, then ran with honesty. 'You're right about everything.'

'What are you going to do about Tamara?'

He was already looking at the bag he'd unpacked the moment he got home. 'Go talk to her.'

'At last, the man has seen sense.' The phone went dead.

Fergus stared at it, a smile starting to spread across his face. He might not have a chance in hell of winning Tamara back, but he was going to give it all he had and more.

The doorbell rang, cutting through the silence enveloping Tamara as she sat at the counter nibbling half-heartedly at a slice of toast. Who could that be? The only people who visited her usually just walked on in, calling out to her.

She didn't recognise the car in the driveway.

The bell rang again.

'Coming,' she muttered, though she'd prefer to ignore it and pretend she wasn't here. There'd been little sleep going on last night, her head a miserable whir of Fergus and what she'd lost.

Hauling the door wide, she did a double take. Couldn't be. She was hallucinating. 'Fergus?'

'Hello, Tamara. Can I come in?'

Had he come to tell her he wanted no part of her in his life? That they wouldn't even be catching up at Christmas? She'd already assumed that to bc the case, and surely, he could've done that on the phone, anyway. But she didn't think he'd come to open up and be completely honest about his feelings. Not after he'd walked away from her yesterday like she didn't matter at all. She looked at him as he waited patiently for her answer. Could she let him in and listen to what he had to say when she doubted it was for her own good? She had no choice. Despite everything, she loved Fergus with all she had.

Her hands were shaking as she stepped back. 'Come in.' He looked tired, as though, like her, he hadn't slept all night.

Stepping past her, he waited until she closed the door. He still wasn't saying much.

'Come through to the kitchen. I've just made coffee.' She led the way, aware of him right behind her every step. Pointing to the stools at the counter, she said, 'Take a pew.'

Fergus hesitated. 'I'm sorry to turn up unannounced, but once I made up my mind to see you, I had to come.'

She hadn't tied back her hair, and it flicked from side to side as she shook her head. 'You didn't want me doing a runner, you mean.' It was there in his wary eyes, in the way he clenched his jaw.

'I had to see you.'

'Had to? Or have to?' Yes, she was being blunt, but how else could she protect herself? She had no idea why Fergus was here. He'd said his bit at the airport. Or so she'd thought.

'Have to,' he conceded, raising a hint of hope in her heart.

But until he said what he'd come for, she was going to hold on to her emotions, not spill them out in a rush for him to walk away from—again. She poured coffee for both of them, then paced back and forth behind the kitchen counter, not knowing what she was waiting for, only that it was going to be big, one way or the other. Finally, she stopped and locked a steady gaze on him. 'Fergus, this waiting is hard.' Then she went back to waiting. Afraid to say another word in case she said the wrong thing and he walked out.

Fergus's shoulders rose and his chest lifted as he drew a long, shaky breath. 'Tamara, I love you.' There, he'd done it. Told Tamara he loved her. So far, the floor was still under his feet.

She was staring at him. 'You what?'

'I see you for who you are, and you're amazing. You always were. I admit that back when we weren't exactly the best of friends, I had the hots for you, but for some reason I've never worked out I didn't want you to be just another notch on my bedpost and nothing else.' Bile soured his mouth. He had been awful to her. 'Tamara—'

'Wait. My turn.' She looked flustered. About to tell him to take a hike and don't come back?

His heart crunched. Not that. He'd finally opened up. There was a lot more still to come. 'I understand I need to be open with you about everything if we're going to make this work.' He stopped. Then the words spilled out, almost unbidden. 'I am so afraid of being hurt again by someone special to me. Apart from Kelvin, all my friends became nightmares, taunting me about my father and what would I do since the money I loved to flaunt had gone. Worse, my mother didn't know how to handle the situation, and apart from offering for me to go to Auckland with her, she got on with her own life by finding someone else to marry and support her. I can't blame her, but I needed her. I'd lost my father, who wasn't the man I'd believed in and loved. That man hadn't ever existed. He'd been a dream, and the dream was gone, destroyed forever.' He gulped down a mouthful of the coffee she'd poured him. Couldn't look at Tamara for fear of what was showing in her face. 'Then I met Harriet and everything was wonderful again. I truly believed, when she agreed to marry me, that I had moved on to a new, more loving life. I was so wrong. Harriet's parents refused to accept that my family history wouldn't destroy her life or those of any children we might've had. At first, she denied that was true, but after a constant barrage from her parents, she gave in and agreed they might be right about us ending our engagement.' He wasn't stopping now. 'I closed down after that. Haven't wanted a relationship since, because I didn't want to go through that pain again.'

'Fergus—'

He held his hand up. He had to finish what he'd started. 'Wait. Then you came back into my life and everything changed. I mean *everything*. I started to feel again. To hope I could love and be loved. To start longing for children and watch them grow up to be stable adults, the best versions of themselves. All because of you, Tamara. I fought it. But I lost. I love you with my heart and soul. You are incredibly special. You arc the one. The only one for me. If you'll have me.' He finally puttered to a stop, unable to utter another word.

Sinking onto a stool, she looked at him with what he thought might be love in her warm gaze. 'I haven't told you much about my past either. When my husband left me, he said I was cold in bed and uncaring about his feelings. I tried not to believe him, but sometimes it was so hard, thinking that was why he didn't love me anymore, and why he cheated on me with an old girlfriend of his.'

He couldn't listen to her pain. Moving around the bench he went to hold her, but she pushed him back with her hand. 'I haven't finished. I loved John, and thought we had the dream life. I was wrong. For a long time, I didn't want to try again, didn't want to have my face rubbed in my own failure.' Another deep breath before she continued. 'Then I caught up with you and like you, I started to look at things differently. Especially you. You have changed and that took guts and determination. Then there're all the other wonderful things about you, like how you treat me, and how you stuck by me during the days after the earthquake. How you worship me in bed. I could go on and on, but it's probably best I shut up now. Other than to tell you—I love you, Fergus Collier. Maybe I always have, though I didn't recognise the heat you created within me as love.' She sat watching him, like she was waiting for an axe to fall.

He couldn't take his eyes off this wonderful woman. She'd always been honest, but this took the cake. She loved him. Unbelievable. Yet true. He stepped up mentally. 'Tamara, I've been falling deeper in love with you every day since we met again at the airport just over a month ago. And for the record, you are not cold, in bed or out of it. You are hot and sexy and gorgeous.' He'd throttle the bastard if he ever met him.

Relief filtered through Tamara's eyes as she took in what he'd said. Coming round the bench, she wrapped him in her arms. 'Take me to bed, Fergus.'

'That's it?' He couldn't stop the smile widening his lips. 'You have nothing more to say?' No wonder he loved her.

'What is there to say? You can trust me to always love you as I trust you to do the same.'

There *was* one more thing to say. It felt so right after all this time holding on to his heart. Taking Tamara's hands in his, he got down on one knee. 'Tamara Frost, will you marry me? Be my forever woman? Have children with me?'

She blinked and a tear slid out of the corner of her eye. 'Yes, Fergus. I will.'

He was on his feet and reaching for her. 'Thank you. That's the best thing I've heard in a long time.'

'We took our time getting here, but I believe that's been for the best. I love you, and probably always have.' Tears were gushing down her face now. 'I can't imagine a life without you now.'

'Then what are we standing around here for? Where's the bedroom?' He scooped her up in his arms, his heart going so fast there was an actual, physical ache behind his ribs. A good ache. His life had come full circle and he was happy beyond belief.

EPILOGUE

Two years later...

TAMARA SAT ON the beach at Port Vila, keeping a constant eye on her daughter, who loved nothing more than to toddle down the few metres to the water's edge and sit down in the water. 'Izzy, be careful, sweetheart.' As if eighteen-month-olds knew what being careful meant.

'Good luck with that.' Fergus grinned. 'She's a water baby.'

'Don't I know it.' Glancing over at the man she'd married seven days ago at the resort where they'd made love for the very first time, she felt her heart go all mushy. 'I can't believe we're here again.' They'd been back once to finish the list interrupted by the earthquake, and then again last year to help more women with gynaecological problems, so when it came to their wedding, it was a no brainer where to hold it.

'This time it's all about wedding bells.'

She nudged him. 'And children.'

Fergus laid his hand over her slight baby bump. ‘Wonder if he knows he was just at his parents’ wedding?’

‘You can ask him in five months’ time.’ She still struggled to get her head around the fact she and Fergus were married and expecting their second child in the middle of next year. Life had really proved to be wonderful. She couldn’t be happier.

‘Izzy, come and give your dad a hug.’ Fergus was watching her as she sat smacking the wet sand. ‘I want her away from the water while I kiss you.’

Tamara laughed. ‘Good luck with that. It’s as though Izzy knows exactly what you’re doing.’

‘She’s no slug. A lot like her mother.’

‘And her father.’ Izzy had stood up and was starting to race up the beach towards them. ‘Quick. We’ve about ten seconds before we’re interrupted.’

As Fergus’s lips covered hers, she sighed with pleasure. When he lifted his mouth, she murmured, ‘I love you, Fergus Collier.’

‘Love you back, Tamara Collier.’

Izzy jumped on Fergus’s back shrieking, ‘Dada!’

Darn, but life was perfect.

* * * * *

If you enjoyed this story, check out these other great reads from Sue MacKay

A Fling with the ER Doctor
Parisian Surgeon's Secret Child
Wedding Date with the ER Doctor
Brooding Vet for the Wallflower

All available now!